ELLIE QUIN SERIES:

THE WORLD ACCORDING TO ELLIE QUIN

Published by Grrr Books, 2012

First Edition

ISBN: 978-0-9575160-1-4

THE WORLD ACCORDING TO ELLIE QUIN
(Book 2 of the Ellie Quin Series)

BY

Alex Scarrow

[Begin...]

[An Audio fragment]:

'...Sorry it's been so long since I last wrote to you Hufty. The first day I arrived here at New Haven I was *razzed* by some off-worlder. I lost everything except this voice-diary and the ID card I got given when I entered. You know, I was all set to turn around and head back home after that, but I don't suppose I'd have been able to make it far without a single cred.'

'But then you know what? It's funny when I think about it, she scared me when I first saw her...this girl picked me up, she saved me, like a knight in shining vinyl. I wish you could meet her, she's so, I don't know, so....fearless, so full of self confidence. I know this may sound strange, and really, I barely know her, but I feel safe when she's around, like nothing can hurt me because she's there. Stupid isn't it?...'

[End of Audio fragment]:

1

OMNIPEDIA:
[Human Universe digital encyclopaedia]

Article: 'The Legend of Ellie Quin'

The audio fragment above is one which has been fully authenticated by voice-print analysis as a genuine diary recording made by Ellie Quin. It is thought she made this entry not long after entering the city of New Haven. Details of this part of her life are rare and sketchy at best. Eight hundred years later all we have are rumours, fairy-tales, myths peddled by many different interest groups - even religions - hoping to co-opt her story in order to support their belief systems or vested interests.

A discerning student of the Legend of Ellie Quin, is best advised to treat with a healthy dose of scepticism most if not all of the anecdotal tales from her time living in the city of New Haven. Many of the myths and tales of her time living there are mere flights of fancy **[Reference-links:] Ellie Quin: The Queen of Aliens. Ellie Quin: The Third and Final Prophet. Ellie Quin and the Seven Mutants]** and have merged into popular culture and mythology. Many of them even appearing in supposedly respected historical d-books, the insta-web, even repositories of open-source knowledge like the Omnipedia. One is best treating all information from this chapter in her life as suspect.

Who really knows what happened to her in there? All we do know for certain is this; at roughly the same time she left home for New Haven, the Administration became aware of her existence and what she could possibly mean to Human Space.

She was an experiment; the creation of a geneticist who had recently died. She was an experiment; a quite deadly experiment and the Administration were very, very frightened. Which is why records indicate one of their very best 'finger men' was immediately dispatched to the labs of the Department of Genetic Analysis to investigate the case and, if necessary, terminate the experiment.'

User Comment > Digi-EeZee
Okay, that's assumption right there. No one knows that for sure.

User Comment > QumpFan

3

Oh? You an expert on Administration-era history are you?

User Comment > Zee-Galactik-Razcal
They sent people to kill her u kno? Thadz wot my brudder sez. Boishee!!!! The Admin wuz like the weevil empire orsumfin.

CHAPTER 1

The shuttle came to rest in landing bay seven, the one used for routine supply deliveries for the Department's laboratories - the 'Meat Library'. It was a discreet arrival, specifically called ahead by the important passenger aboard – the man from the Administration, a man in his late thirties, and arguably at the top of his game.

Deacon.

As the clouds of coolant steam thinned and cleared from the pad, the exit ramp dropped lightly onto the deck. He emerged from the shuttle holding a small travel bag in one hand. Deacon liked to travel light; a change or two of clothes, some toiletries, a good antique, *paper*, book to read and that was all. It kept things simple if he was going to be on the move a lot; and it certainly seemed that was going to be the way things were for him for the foreseeable future.

He looked around the landing bay. No welcome party of high-ranking Department bureaucrats waiting to greet him. Just as he'd hoped.

'Jolly good,' he uttered. Discretion was everything.

He turned around to beckon over the nervous and agitated young man who was hovering just inside the shuttle.

'It's okay Leonard, it's quite safe,' he cajoled gently.

Leonard took several tentative steps down the ramp to join Deacon.

'Leonard, we need to make a start immediately. We need to go through all of Mason's files. I want you going through his notes, see if you can find anything that's going to give us a lead.'

'Y-yes sir.'

'I'll find the acting department head, and let him know we're here,' added Deacon. He stroked the dark bristles of the tightly clipped beard and moustache that ran a thin pencil-line around his mouth. He knew Mason's deputy, and now acting department head, was a characterless pen-pusher. The man would do anything he could to co-operate after Deacon announced where he had flown in from and the source of his authority.

He strode stiffly across the deserted landing deck, the forefinger of one hand tucked smartly into his expensively tailored, *genuine* silk waistcoat, as if in the act of retrieving a fob watch. His dark, three-quarter length evening jacket flapped with each vigorous stride. Lenny followed in his wake, anxiously glancing around the echoing cavernous bay interior.

*

Deacon settled into Mason's chair and spun it immediately around to stare out of the window, down onto the spectacular cerulean world of Pacifica.

A lovely view.

He envied the old man that; the view. Deacon's own world - *Liberty*, the seat of government - was predominantly urban. It was the base world for the Colonial Administration's various departments and the extensive administrative core. A densely populated world with only tiny areas of wilderness left untouched and preserved in roofed-over terrariums, for those willing to pay enough to enjoy the sensation of grass beneath their toes; the hiss of leaves stirring on branches. Beyond those exclusive biomes of nature, it was a noisy bustling world of plastex and carbocrete.

Certainly no wilderness, no empty spaces, no babbling brook beside which a man might order his thoughts. Not on Liberty.

He smiled as he savoured the beautiful view. By contrast, Pacifica was refreshingly empty, a world of flat horizons and a sky almost free of the orbital clutter of mankind. Only the more observant of the few hundred thousand inhabitants down there, living on small man-made floating villages, might notice the three larger stars in their night sky, moving slowly to keep a geo-stationary orbit - the laboratory, and her two, ever-present, military escort ships.

When this was all over, and that might take some time he suspected, Deacon promised himself he would take a sabbatical for a few years and enjoy some solitude down there on that peaceful water-world. He was long overdue time away from the constant gibbering white noise of people. Deacon needed that, every so often, a little time away from the herd.

He turned round to face Mason's desk. Deacon respected the old man's taste for early twentieth century furniture. The hue of the faux-wood in the natural light reflected from Pacifica was rich and auburn. In another time, under different circumstances, he could imagine Dr Mason and himself as fellow enthusiasts, fellow collectors, perhaps even being friends, sharing as they did a very uncommon and very unfashionable admiration for Old Earth antiques.

Deacon cringed with revulsion at what the great unwashed masses of humankind considered *good taste* these days; baggy, formless, untailored, neon coloured clothes, ultra-minimal silver and chrome finished furniture, glistening, plastic, chunky gold-painted jewellery. The vulgarity of people's taste turned his stomach. Since being a boy he had preferred the muted dignity of dark and rich deep colours; burgundy, navy blue, jade green, and had a taste for the elegant contours of early twentieth century couture. His suit, a rendition of Edwardian English style, hugged his lean, well toned body tightly. He had no need for bulging thigh pockets, puffy airbag jackets or oversized and sagging pants to hide the sagging cellulite amassed from too many junk food meals.

But then, all of that might change if Mason's creature destroyed the universe.

Deacon was almost tempted to let Mason's plan run its course. Perhaps the universe might be a better place without human trailer trash littering it with their habi-cubes, food wrappers and awful pounding music.

But it would also lead to unfathomable chaos, the end of the Administration and order - a return to darker days. Mason's child, his creature, his genetic abomination had to be found at any cost. His briefing back on Liberty, directly face to face with no less than three of the ruling committee, had been unequivocal;

You have the highest authority in this matter. The child must be found and destroyed.

Deacon knew they had to act swiftly. And he suspected that somewhere in this study or in Mason's personal data space would lie a clue that would lead them directly to this child.

And Lenny, his assistant, would surely find it.

He looked up at the young lad, standing quietly beyond the desk and staring wide-eyed out of the window at the blue world outside.

'Come, sit down here Lenny,' Deacon said, standing up and offering him Mason's chair. Lenny shuffled awkwardly around and settled into the chair, as Deacon swiped a hand over the desk lens and the holo-screen flickered on in front of them.

'Dr Mason was a genius Lenny, but also quite a bit careless. His thoughts, his conclusions and his plan are all in here, spelled out in great detail. But the one thing I'm certain he would have been so careful never to enter as digital data, was the code number or location of this child. We need to know where it is, Lenny.'

'Yes Sir.'

'Do what you do best, lad. Help me find it.'

Lenny smiled. Nothing satisfied him more than to be able to please his mentor.

CHAPTER 2

'New Haven can be quite a scary place if you don't know it too well. The first day I arrived, even before I was razzed, I'll be honest, I was petrified by it. And if I'm really honest with myself now, even if I hadn't lost everything on that first day, I wonder whether I would have lasted even a week in this place if it hadn't been for her.'

Ellie snapped off the voice diary, suddenly aware that she was thirsty. She sat up in bed, nearly hitting her head on the storage unit above it. She looked around her bedpod with some degree of satisfaction. Okay, so it was small, in fact it was a quarter of the size of the habi-cube she slept in back…*home*. Ellie realised the word 'home' had come with the slightest hesitation. The farm, Mum, Dad, Ted and Shona, that would always be 'home', but after only these three weeks, the small contained flat she shared with Jez was beginning to feel like a home too. The walls of her cube were plain white, unadorned with decoration or colour, unlike Jez's, which were adorned with pictures of semi-naked men and some women…and some halfway in between; most of them genetically enhanced to feature bulging pants and/or improbably large breasts.

She stood up in the two-foot margin alongside her cushi-bunk. That was it for floor space in her bedpod; two feet by five. She pulled some clothes out of the storage unit above her bunk to throw over her underwear. Jez of course, was quite happy parading around unashamedly in their small habi-flat wearing a thong and a 'top' that was not much more than a nipple-covering elastex band. Of course, Jez knew she had a body with remarkably attractive athletic contours and had the irritating habit of loitering in front of anything that vaguely reflected her Amazonian gorgeousness back at her. Ellie on the other hand looked down at her whippet-thin body and catalogued her small list of woes; knobbly knees, drainpipe-hips, mouse-breasts and the still visible, but fading rash from those tubweed stings on her forearms. She pulled nylo leggings over her feet and up her narrow hips and threw on the other things that were tangled in the pile of clothes. She looked in a small mirror. Her face was still blotched with the makeup they'd been playing around with last night.

Good enough.

She picked up the voice diary and squeezed past the bunk to leave her pod.

'The habi-flat we're sharing is kinda tight. I mean re-e-eally tight. One bedpod for her, one for me, there's a washroom the size of a coffin and a shared area where we kind of do everything else,' she muttered quietly into the diary as she entered the main space.

'Jez's asleep right now I think. She had a heavy session last night. She brought a man back and drank quite a few Spartans. I think she kicked him out sometime during the night.'

Ellie suspected Jez wasn't the easiest person to share a bed with while suffering a hangover.

Ellie wandered across the small communal space; not much 'wandering' going on though; five steps and you were across it. On one wall was the suggestion of a 'kitchen'; little more than a fridge, a FoodSmart and a small tap and basin. In the middle of the room was a single gel-couch facing a small, second hand holovee projector.

'We've got a skanky old toob we bought for only a few creds. Would you believe it, Hufty…I've actually taken to watching the sopa-drams? That is when I'm not working,

14

or she hasn't dragged me out to yet another crazy go-juice joint.'

Mum watched them, Shona too. That used to really bug the Hell out of Ellie, the pair of them watching all that ditto-head crap. Always the same stock characters, always facing the same emotional dilemmas, or fighting or carrying on some ridiculous feud with some other character that goes on and on from episode to episode.

'Jez really loves 'em. She forced me to sit down with her and watch an episode of one of them from beginning to end. What was it called...? Oh yeah *Shuttle Stop 12*.' It was a sopa-dram set in one of the type of shuttle-stopovers dotted around Harpers Reach; the usual collection of stereotypes playing the pilot, the engineer, the canteen cook, the storekeeper and the other regular characters. And then there were the passengers that passed through, the grumpy ones, the mysterious ones, the romantic ones; life's rich cast of soap opera clichés

Ellie opened the fridge and pulled out a box of Solar Nuggatz and poured herself a bowl. This particular box had contained a 'Plaz' - the red Plasma Ranger, it stood on top of the FoodSmart.

'I guess I've got *her* to thank for that, now I'm hooked into watching that stupid Shuttle show whenever it's on.'

She poured some soyo-milk over the cereal and instinctively switched on the toob before flopping down onto the gel-couch to eat her breakfast. It was early yet and the only programs on were newsie shows and Quizzers. She shuffled through a dozen stations before giving up, muting the toob and speaking into her diary once more.

'I've got a job. I started it last week. Okay. It's not the greatest job in the world, but it's enough creds that I can pay my share on the habi', and have enough over. I'm cooking in a Slap'n'Grill over in the Industrial Sector. It's thirty minutes across the city in a skyhound which isn't too bad, I guess. But, Hufty, the food I have to cook up is just totally gaggo. There's a lot of off-world types working in the Industrial Sector, so this place does native food for them…and *boishee*…' she curled her lips, 'some of it is pretty gross.'

'Well Hufty, I gotta go. It's a work-day today and I need to be dressed and on my way pretty soon. I guess you can see that things are working out pretty good, and they'll get better. I promise I won't leave it so long next time.'

She snapped off the diary once more and finished off her breakfast, slurping the last of the soyo-milk from the bowl.

CHAPTER 3

She exited through the double perspex doors of the tower onto the upper-level pedestrian walkway linking their scruffy, billboard-encrusted tower with a neighbouring one and waited in the bubble-stop half way along for the skyhound. This morning she was up and out three quarters of an hour earlier than usual for a work-day. It was dawn-minus-one, six o'clock in quaint Old Earth dialect – the way Dad would say it. She was anxious to make sure she managed to keep the rendezvous she'd arranged three weeks ago with Aaron Goodman.

Through the semi-opaque plexitex sky overhead, she could just make out the peach colour of the predawn sky replacing the purple of night. The city was quiet at this hour. The incessant rumble of sky-car traffic, the bass throbbing of music from some street levels below, the irritating repetition of slogans and catchphrases from the larger advertising screens and the floating billboards, the half-hourly rooftop call-to-prayer of Chrislamists; all of that was absent at this peaceful hour.

She sheltered inside the bubble stop from the gusting, cool winds that blew around the tops of the towers. The people who lived up here at the top called it the 'hurling'. It was New Haven's own, unintended, weather system; convection currents of the warm air from street level gusting up and displacing the cooler air at the top.

From here she could see a sizeable portion of the city. Many of the tall tenement towers were dark twilight pepper-pot silhouettes; a few round habi-flat portholes glowed with other early risers. But in the large the buildings were dark slabs. A couple of hours from now, the billboards that encrusted them would flicker and stir to life; become a patchwork quilt of neon coloured commercials.

Far below at street level, the pedestrian walkways were empty. Here and there bathed in weak pools of cyan coloured from the night-light globes, She spotted the faint stirring of some poor homeless bastard, pulling a rag blanket over himself to stay warm.

That so could have been me.

She heard the whine of a single sky-car pass over, its headlights flickered over the bubble, momentarily dazzling her. It passed by smoothly, untroubled by airborne gridlock and she watched it become a mere dot in the distance, and disappear as it dived down steeply to the cityscape below. Ellie wondered what it must be like to be one of the rich few who could afford to drive those inside New Haven. The purchase tax alone on those vehicles was as much as buying a decent sized habi-flat. She spotted another one far away, its twin front lights twinkled like two faint stars tethered together.

Now *that* was something she missed…seeing the night sky clearly; the infinite glittering of stars, the golden slash, the rich purple of the sky, the movement of interstellar ships out there beyond this world's thin atmosphere. The little porthole of her own bedpod was angled downwards so that her limited view was of the streets far below. The same with most of the other habi-flat windows. Like a million beady eyes, all of them gazing downward. A design feature; people like to gaze down on the homeless; on the heaving stew of life below.

Who wants to look at boring fregging stars, right?

Another beam of light flickered across the bubble-stop and Ellie saw the large yellow drink-bottle shape of the skyhound descending as it approached her. Thrusters hissed as it decreased speed, gently bumped against the walkway, and locked itself against the bubble stop with a gentle thud. An opening appeared in the plastic as a passenger door slid open on the side of the hound and she stepped in, displaying her ID card to a scanner. A holographic display indicated a deduction of 1.25C.

The skyhound was empty.

She stood towards the back of it, where the carbo-steel hull gave way to a plexitex viewing blister. Watching the city pass beneath and recede smoothly was normally how she preferred to spend her journey across New Haven to the Industrial Sector. This morning, however, she was on her way to the South entrance, only a couple of stops beyond where she normally climbed off the hound and made her way down to street level in order to complete her journey to work on foot.

I wonder how Sean is doing?

That one came entirely out of nowhere; she realised that she hadn't spared him a thought since she'd moved in with Jez. She felt a puzzling mixture of guilt and something like pride.

Guilt.

She owed him more than this; more than just dismissing him from her mind like she'd done over the last three weeks. But then she knew Sean would be so proud of her.

She guessed that the Freezer would be well on its way out of the Seventh Veil and racing home at great speed across the vast empty space between systems to their training planet, GL5-D. She tried to imagine him locked inside his own sarcophagus, awake, thinking, albeit incredibly slowly, about home. She imagined him dreamily contemplating the exciting challenges that were awaiting him, perhaps, possibly sparing a thought for her in return. Quite possibly, in that dreamy slow motion existence; worrying about how she was faring alone in New Haven?

She desperately hoped that she'd not caused him any trouble with his father attempting to contact him aboard the Freezer to ask him if he knew of her whereabouts.

She played with a scenario. What if Sean turned up right now. Appeared right now on this skyhound and asked her to marry him and settle down on some agri-plot out there in that clay wilderness?

The farm. Raise a crop of plant-animals. Maybe put in for a child or three? She could see herself becoming mum. A world of three domes and a once-a-year trip to a trade show.

She answered her hypothetical scenario very quickly.

No, thanks.

The life she was leading right now was what she wanted. At least for now. The work she had was pretty dag, but it was bringing in the creds, and living life with Jez was fun. Plain and simple. Ellie wasn't ever going to admit to her cube-mate that she was the first proper 'girl' friend she'd ever had. That would sound so sad, so pathetic, so like her. In fact Ellie had so far been very coy about telling Jez about her life before New Haven. All she'd told her was what she'd figured within minutes of meeting her; a farm girl drawn to the big shiny city. That's it. It was enough for Jez.

Things have changed so much, so quickly.

She had moved into that cube three weeks ago with absolutely nothing. Jez said that she'd been sharing the cube with another girl who had upped and left with no warning, leaving her in a tangle with a rent she couldn't afford on her own. So, Jez had said, actually it was a mutually beneficial arrangement to both of them; not an act of charity.

She had offered to cover Ellie's first month of rent, to give her time to find a job and get established. Then of course, she could fregging-well start paying her half.

That very first night in the habi-flat? They'd stayed in. Jez had whipped up some savoury gunk in the FoodSmart, produced a few bottles of Lemon-Bubba and they ate, talked, drank and giggled (after a couple of bottles each) until the early hours of the morning.

Ellie figured, as she nursed her first ever hangover the next morning, that things were going to turn out just fine.

The skyhound descended several hundred feet as it passed over the Industrial Sector and approached the South entrance. The ceiling height was lowering as they approached the edge of the city and the huge plexitex dome above them began to slope down to meet the ground.

Ellie could just about see the outline of the landing fields through the fogginess of the plastic shield and wondered if *Lisa* was parked out there on one of the green pads. She hoped Aaron was already down and grabbing an unhealthy breakfast at Dionysius. She wouldn't be able to stay long, perhaps ten, maybe twenty minutes, then she'd need to make her way back on foot to the Industrial Sector to start her morning shift.

The skyhound was beginning to fill up with people starting their commute to work, and she was relieved when it finally descended to street level near the plaza she'd stood on when she'd first entered New Haven three weeks ago.

Seems like ages ago now.

Just three weeks, and all of a sudden, the previous nineteen years she'd lived on Harpers Reach felt almost like *somebody else's* life.

She hopped out on to the street, fighting against a surge of people trying to get on the hound, and made her way up the wide thoroughfare towards the small, unremarkable bulkhead that opened onto the immigration centre; New Haven's busiest entry point.

She walked past it, noticing a small family, a young couple with a boy a little younger than Ted, staring up in awe and with some degree of trepidation.

She grinned. *Newcomer, eh? Pfttt.*

She hoped they weren't going to be razzed on their first day and lose everything like she had. It was a grim reality of life, she pondered, that there wouldn't be a Jez; a knight-ess in shining armour, out there to pick up every newcomer who came badly unwrapped on their first day.

She proceeded across the plaza, picking up her pace as she spotted the canteen. It was cluttered with grimy, unshaven men in oily dirty overalls. Pilots like Aaron, stopping here long enough to deliver and collect, and grab a fried breakfast of fat-soaked synthi meat. She scanned the various men digging into steaming plates of food, but saw no sign of him. She weaved through the plastic chairs to the door of the canteen and opened it. Inside a warm fog of steamed food and body odour greeted her. A familiar smell, not so different to that of the kitchen in which she worked. She studied the queue of men by the counter, many of whom turned to stare at her in a way she found uncomfortable; in the same way they looked hungrily at their freshly fried food.

There was no sign of him inside.

She decided her best bet was to take a seat at one of the tables outside the diner and watch for him. She could do that for only another fifteen or twenty minutes, then she knew, regretfully, she would really have to get on her way to work. Ellie picked an empty table and made her way over to it. She pushed to one side the detritus on the table to one side; an empty plate with scraps and a cup with the dregs of a coffee in the bottom. She was wrestling with a chair, awkwardly wedged beneath a table, when she felt a heavy thud on her narrow back.

CHAPTER 4

'Hey Ellie girl? Good God, is that you?' rumbled Aaron, looking down at her, his face a mask of surprise.

'Aaron!' she cried, surprised at how delighted she was to see his scruffy face once more. She embraced him, wrapping her arms around his broad shoulders. He swamped her awkwardly with one large arm in return, and then held her away from him to look at her. 'What's happened to you?' he said with incredulity.

She didn't understand at first, but then it occurred to her that she must look radically different to the girl he'd dropped off three weeks ago.

Jez's influence of course.

She had taken Ellie round some market stalls selling cheap off-world clothes, selecting garments that were more to *her* taste than Ellie's. She'd also gone to great pains to show her how to apply make-up, again in off-world fashion; pale foundation, dark eye shadow and carbon-black lipstick. By the time she had finished, Ellie looked like a hastily assembled, down-market version of Jez.

Aaron gazed at her death mask make-up and her dyed, fox-red hair , the black vinyl thigh-boots, the pink lace tutu skirt under a dark green pvc corset...and the Crazie-Beanie T-shirt. He took it all in with an expression of disapproval and concern.

'Oh yes,' she shrugged self-consciously, 'I...I've got a bunch of new clothes now,' she said offering a smile that looked like an apology.

'I noticed,' he said. 'Sit down, I'll go and get us some coffee. Then you can tell me what the Hell you've been up to these last few weeks.'

'Okay,' she said. She got the idea he disapproved as she watched him head inside the canteen. He was gone for only a few minutes before returning with two plates of steaming food and a couple of plyfoam cups of coffee on a tray.

'Oh....I'm not *that* hungry,' she said curling her black-painted lips in disgust as she studied the pool of fat-soaked food on the plate he set down in front of her.

'You look like you could do with some decent food, girl. So eat up.'

Ellie's stomach churned at the thought of placing that food in her mouth, but at the same time she didn't want to start off on a bad vibe with Aaron. 'Okay,' she said picking up a plastic fork and starting to push the fried synthi meat around unenthusiastically.

'So, how have you been getting on?' he asked.

'Fine, I guess.'

'Fine eh? So you got some new clothes. I guess you've got the other, more important things covered then, like somewhere to stay?…a job? Right?'

Ellie nodded. 'Oh, yes. Covered. I'm doing okay. I'm sharing a cube with another girl, I've got a job.'

'A job?' he said with surprise and a genuine smile of approval. 'What is it?'

'Uh…it's umm in catering.'

Aaron prodded a fork at his food. 'In *catering* huh? Posh tucker is it? I suppose you probably look down on gunk like this now, eh?'

You kidding? I make gunk like this now.

'Yeah,' she answered reluctantly.

'So, tell me about the girl that you're living with?'

30

She wondered how true an answer she could give Aaron. There seemed to be so much that would need to be edited out of an honest answer that she might as well lie to him. She didn't want Aaron to know that Jez was an exotic dancer in one of the seediest flesh bars in the Service Sector. That she brought home men on a regular basis and often made enough noise in her cube that Ellie sometimes slept with headphones on. That wasn't what he looked like he wanted to hear from her right now.

'She's quiet, you know, shy....not a lot of trouble really.'

'Uh huh. She's like you, eh? Another runaway?'

Ellie knew virtually nothing about Jez's past. 'Yeah, another farm girl like me,' she said with what she hoped was a reassuring smile. 'But she's been here a bit longer, so she's helped me find my way around.'

'That's good,' he said nodding, chomping on a mouthful of synthetic fat and gristle. 'How old is she?'

Ellie shuffled uncomfortably. Jez was twenty-six, six years older; the difference between being kidult and an adult.

'Umm, a couple of years older I guess,' she muttered quietly. She hated lying to him, especially after all the kindness he'd shown her.

Aaron continued eating in silence, shovelling the food into his mouth briskly. 'A little older, eh?' he said eventually. 'And she's the one I guess who's been handing out the fashion tips, hmmm?'

Ellie nodded.

'Well, it seems like I needn't have worried so much about you over the last three weeks then,' he said. 'It looks like you've adjusted quickly. Maybe you really are the city type.'

Ellie thought she detected to tone of reproach in his voice. 'Yes, I'm doing alright, I guess.'

She wondered whether to tell him about what happened to the money he had loaned her, tell him how she was mugged on the first day and lost it all. But if she told him, maybe he would think she was lying, maybe he would think she was hoping he would let her off the payback by telling him such a story. She'd hate that - him thinking that of her. She was determined to pay him back.

'Aaron, about the money…'

'Oh, yeah. Forgive me for sneaking that letter into your bag. I just wanted to be sure you had enough-'

'Thank you, Aaron. It really helped me a lot!'

I wish.

'But I just wanted to say, I'll pay you back. I promise.'

'Okay Ellie, don't sweat it. When you can, you can. But listen, how can I say this?' Aaron put down his knife and fork and steepled his fingers beneath his unshaven chin as he searched for the right words to carry on.

'I'll be honest…I'm a bit concerned about you already girl,' he said studying her. 'You know what you look like right now?'

Ellie didn't like the sound of where this was going. 'Fashionable?'

He sniffed. Was that a laugh?

'Maybe,' he sighed. 'I wouldn't even begin to know what's fregging fashionable. But if you asked me, I'd say you look a little like one of those poor bitches that work the flesh bars. All dressed up like a pleasure-doll or some piece of meat in a grunt-flik. You're barely more than a child, Ellie.'

'I'm twenty!' Ellie felt her face burn hot underneath the caked-on makeup. 'I'm allowed to do what I want now. And anyway, who the Hell made you my Dad all of a sudden?'

Aaron's face dropped and, for the first time, his gruff sandblasted demeanour revealed a fragile fissure. That outburst had stung him.

'Hey...I'm worried is all, Ellie. You've been here three weeks, and already this city has got its hooks into you. You're already dressing like the deadheads that shuffle round this place. No. Worse than that, you're dressing like the kind of whore who picks up the deadheads that shuffle-'

She spurted coffee. 'What?!'

'How long before this place totally sucks you in, huh? And you end up-'

'How I dress is my business, Aaron!'

'...and you end up, just another waster. A dome-drone, living your life through the toob, or worse, spending all you earn tossing chemical shit down your throat it in one of those bars.'

'I don't believe this! I dye my hair and buy a few clothes, and you're saying all these nasty things!' Her voice was wobbling. Her anger was swiftly escalating toward tears. Damned if she was going to do that. Blub like a girl.

'Ellie, *Christ*...you need to get out now, before this city swallows you up and turns you into another one of them,' he said, pointing to the brightly coloured pedestrians shuffling past nearby. 'Look,' he added, lowering his voice, 'I'm doing a polar run tomorrow. Come with me and let's see the snow again huh? We'll make another snowman, a bigger one this time, and have a snowball fight.'

Ellie was tempted by that, by the simple, childish, uncomplicated pleasure of it. But she had a toe-hold on the city now, and with Jez by her side she felt almost invincible. Yes that was it. *Invincible.* New Haven was beginning to feel like a playground in which they were both going to have the time of their lives. Exploring the Great Beyond, even heading off-world could wait just a little while, right? It wasn't going anywhere. And, look, it had only been three weeks. No time at all. It felt right. For now.

'Sorry Aaron, I want to stay here.'

Aaron shook his head sadly. 'If you stay here, you'll never get out, Ellie. New Haven will eat you. You'll never get far enough ahead of the game to think about anything other than meeting the rent and the bills. That's how it works here, that's the system.'

'I'm staying,' she answered him.

He pushed his plate away and turned to the coffee. The food no longer seemed quite so appetizing to him. 'Well listen to me here….you owe me eight hundred creds, Ellie. You owe me that money.'

Oh crud! here goes….

'And that's *a lot* of money to find when you're trying to pay for some shitty habi-flat and the weekly O2 bill for the air that you breath, girl. But that's exactly what you've got to do week in and week out in New Haven.'

'Aaron, about the money, on the first day I…'

'No listen to me. You can forget about the loan, write it off okay? But you've got to do me one small favour.'

Ellie looked up at him nervously, she couldn't imagine what he could want that would off-set eight hundred creds. 'What?'

'When I left you on that launch pad, and you were getting ready to enter, you had a goal didn't you? Do you remember that? Beyond getting into the city, you had an aim greater than this, right?'

Ellie nodded slowly. She'd wanted to follow Sean's example.

'I haven't forgotten. Leaving Harpers Reach,' she replied, 'seeing some of the other worlds out there.'

Aaron smiled hopefully. 'Yes. So, I want you to make sure you keep in touch with me. And if you do, I'll see how I can help you get there. I'll keep reminding you of that goal Ellie, nagging you every time we see each other. And you've got to promise not to avoid me, do you understand? Otherwise I'll have my eight hundred creds straight back, or God help you.'

'Okay Aaron,' she said.

'Okay then,' he agreed. 'I'll give you my V.I. number, just for emergencies.'

He handed Ellie a card. It would have to be for emergencies only, the cost of calling him thousands of miles away up at the polar cap, or around on the other side of the planet at Harvest City, would be astronomical.

'But we'll meet here again when I get back in two weeks, same time. And your favour to me will be to make sure you keep coming to see me, every two or three weeks, alright?'

That seemed reasonable to her, given that there was no way she could imagine paying him back from what she earned right now. Or any time soon for that matter. And yes, she owed him this.

'All right.'

'And…you stay in touch with your folks.'

'I've already called them.'

'Good. Well keep doing that. Just a quick call. A credit here, a credit there. That won't break the bank, right?'

She caught a glimpse of the time on an ad-blimp floating high above the skyline. It was half past.

'Oh freg! I've got to go!'

'Your catering job?'

'Yeah,' she said pushing back the plastic chair so quickly it clattered over on to the floor and drew the attention of a group of men shambling by in the street. They wolf-whistled and called out phrases that she was beginning to get used to and normally would have brushed off without a second thought. But in front of Aaron, wearing these clothes, the make-up, she felt exactly like what he'd said; *a pleasure doll*. A cheap one at that.

'You might want to have a little rethink on the fashion clothes Ellie,' he rumbled quietly. 'Tone it down a bit?'

She smiled, nodded. She knew he meant well. 'Okay.' She thumbed over her shoulder. 'Aaron, I'm sorry, I've got to…'

'I know,' he waved her off, 'you go before you're too late. Remember, time moves along a lot quicker than you think.' He gave her a tight smile. 'See you here in a couple of weeks? Don't be late…otherwise you're buying.'

But she was already gone; already swallowed up by the passing current of pedestrians.

OMNIPEDIA:
[Human Universe digital encyclopaedia]

Article: Ellie Quin > Aliens

Of the thirteen hundred worlds within Human Space, records from the thirty-fifth century show that over half had indigenous life of one sort or another on them prior to the arrival of settlers and their terraforming machines. In many cases, the indigenous life were little more than single-cell organisms, but on over two hundred worlds life had developed significantly to produce more complex forms. Nonetheless, many of these species were still primitive.

Seven hundred years ago it appeared that we were the only race with the ability to travel between the stars. But that ended with the first encounters of other intelligent species on far flung worlds at the edge of Human Space. Although these races were all less technologically developed than humankind, they offered fascinating new cultural models, philosophical ideas and sexually transmittable diseases as they began to integrate into the human population.

Of the many alien species that integrated successfully with humans the most enigmatic of them were known by most people by the colloquial name – 'Boojams'.

Boojams, as any young child today can tell you, died out suddenly some three hundred years ago; victims of a virulent plague that passed quickly and easily throughout Human Space, carried by humans and affecting only this unfortunate, fledgling race. Prior to our totally destroying them with what to us was little more than the common cold, they were the first alien race to assimilate on a wide scale into our society and although there are none to be seen today, their elephantine appearance was distinctive. Echoes of their likeness can be seen everywhere today from product logos to children's bedtime stories, where a Boojam, or similar-looking creature, will often play a sympathetic and kindly character with a wealth of old-fashioned, home-spun wisdom and guidance to impart.

The other species that quite often makes an appearance in colonial folk lore were called The 'Onlookers'. At the time of Ellie Quin, this species had only recently been encountered. Back then very little was known about them as emissaries from the

Administration had met only a few dozen times with chosen delegates of theirs. Early commentaries of the time described them as being mobile micro-colonies of less evolved creatures, vaguely reminiscent of frogs. One of the first of our emissaries to meet the Onlookers described them as 'twisting clusters of smooth, olive-skinned creatures, their small limbs and bodies entwined so tightly that they formed a larger, more substantial entity'. As we know from history, it was only shortly after these first few tentative encounters that they revealed their true nature to humankind.

User Comment > XXXAlienzzzzXXX
See hardcore Human-Alien sex vizzees here!!!

User Comment > Feral Master
The alienz on my planet suck. They're stupid [xxxx]ing morons. I throw stones at them and kill them. They're so stupid.

User Comment > Willow-Girl
You're a cruel ignorant [xxxx] dittohead, Feral. I hope one day some aliens come and kill you! Your type make me ashamed to be human.

User Comment > Anonymous

What planet you live on Feral? Maybe same as me? Koodz - they're like big [xxxx]ing slugs. We run over the baby ones and squish them. They squeek just before they pop. Beautiful! Hah! 8D

User Comment > Lay Tawnee

Feral and the poster above DISGUST me! You're no better than animals. I hope some law marshal somewhere is reading this comment thread. You should both be ASHAMED of yourselves!

User Comment > Anonymous

Wah-wah-wah-wah! Listen to Tawnee cry like a big bay-bee. Go [xxxx] yerself you stupid [xxxxxx]

CHAPTER 5

She saw her first alien a few months after arriving in New Haven. Ellie had expected to see them everywhere in the city for some reason, but as yet, very few Boojams seemed to have been enticed into settling down on Harpers Reach. They were a common enough sight on many of the more established colony worlds. She guessed they preferred the comfort and stability of these older, terraformed planets, where the population was more equably dispersed across the entire surface and not crammed together into an enviro-dome.

The evening on which she saw her first ever alien had started ominously. Jez, fuming and spitting venom, had dragged Ellie out of their cube shortly after she had wearily trudged in through the front door, exhausted after a hard day working in the diner. She had grabbed Ellie by the arm, and without a word, marched her down to a small bar at street level. After she had bought a couple of Spartans they found a relatively quiet corner of the bar in which to sit. Ellie decided she'd waited long enough to hear what this was all about.

'Are you going to tell me what's up then?'

'I quit my job.'

'You did what?'

'You heard. I quit that dancing job down at Dantes.'

Exotic dancing . The hours were scandalously easy and the money was great. When Ellie had asked, not long after she'd moved in, whether it was a job she might be able to do too, Jez had gone to great lengths to convince her that it wasn't *that* great a deal; those creepy-looking basket-cases that frequented the place, ogling her body, made her skin crawl, and the fights that broke out occasionally were sometimes unpleasantly close to the dance podiums.

Jez being protective. Jez acting the big sister.

Although it was easy money, the easiest, in fact, she'd insisted that Ellie was way too 'farmy' and innocent to be exposed to that kind of grubbiness. In a way she was glad Jez was trying to discourage her like that. It felt reassuring, comforting. And anyway, Ellie reflected, she probably would be a really cruddy dancer, wriggling

45

unconvincingly, self-consciously and most definitely out of time with the music. Plus of course, who'd want to see her skinny frame almost naked, spasmodically twitching to music?

'Why did you quit?' asked Ellie.

'Because some frecking, slimy-fisted offworlder broke the Look-Don't-Touch rule, once too often.'

Ellie was surprised that she should quit over something as trivial as that. Jez confessed that most nights there were always one or two inebriated punters who pushed their luck a little too far only to have their unwelcome paws slapped casually away. Jez was used to dealing with that.

'You quit because one of them *touched* you?'

'Well,' Jez mumbled guiltily, ' I quit because I broke his arm…by accident, I might add.'

'*What*?'

'The idiot wanted a stroke. Knees down, I'm okay with that. But he was heading up. So I kicked at his stupid arm, and the stupid thing snapped.'

Ellie's bit her lip. 'Crud!'

'So…this guy was going to call in a law marshal, but my oh-so-*loyal* boss, oh

46

yes…my very *loyal* boss, decided to calm him down by sacking me on the spot,' Jez hissed angrily. 'So, I decided the fregging drook wouldn't sack me; I quit instead.' Jez added, nodding her head resolutely. 'That showed him, right?'

Ellie offered a supportive smile. 'I suppose it did. So, what are you going to do now?' she asked.

'Get totally juiced on my last paycheque. I'll worry about it tomorrow.'

Ellie looked out through the grimy, condensation-fogged window of the bar at the passing river of pavement-traffic. So many of them looked drawn and beaten into submission, shambling on their way through the neon-lit murkiness of evening to or from jobs that paid barely enough to keep them in cubes. It dawned on her that her cruddy little job down at the slap 'n' grill wasn't going to keep both of them going for long. Jez's wage had dwarfed hers, and whilst these last few weeks she had just about been able to pay her side of the rent, Jez was the one who paid the O2 bill and for most of the shopping. Unless Jez could find another job as well paid as the one at *Dantes*, pretty soon, the pair of them would be turfed out onto the street. Ellie shuddered at the thought of losing the modest comforts she had only so recently grown accustomed to.

'We'll need to bring in some more money,' she said finally, knowing Jez would curse her at being reminded of the bleeding obvious. 'We can't carry on for long. Not on what I'm earning.'

Jez stared glumly out of the window.

'I can see if I can work some extra shifts there. I'm sure there are some spare hours going,' Ellie added.

'You already work stupidly-long hours there Ellie,' Jez replied, taking a long slurp of her Spartan. 'Is that what we're here for girl? Wake up, go to work, come home, eat, sleep so we're refreshed and ready to do it all again? Is that it?'

'We've got to get some more money, Jez. Otherwise-'

'Yeah, we need money to keep on keeping on. But…but that just sucks. Doesn't it?'

Ellie shrugged. 'What else can we do?'Jez turned and looked at her with disgust. 'Are you serious? Have you been dragged down so fregging quickly? A few weeks ago you were talking to me about leaving Harpers Reach; making it out there into the stars and seeing it all. A real wilderness-chik, a wild-child, girl-with-a-pulse…not like those damned zombies out there. Now, you're looking at me and telling me I should be worrying about paying bills? Ellie girl, you need a wake-up slap.'

Ellie recoiled at Jez's tirade. 'I was just saying we'll need to get some more money or we'll be kicked out of our cube.'

Jez laughed, spurting a cloud of her drink out through her nose. 'Is that ALL there is to worry about!?' She continued in a mewling voice that aped Ellie's out-of-city accent. *'We must have enough to pay the bills*.'

Ellie scowled. Jez was laughing *at* her. She could be thoughtless, thick-skinned, sometimes even downright offensive, but to date, she had never laughed at Ellie. Never derided her. Never looked down at her for being a naïve *farmie*. Ellie wondered if that precedent was about to be set, and whether this little outburst of scorn would prove to be the very beginning of the end of their short friendship as Jez tossed Boring-Pay-The-Bills-Ellie aside to replace her with some other lost sob-story waif to be next month's pet charity project.

'My little cube-buddy,' Jez said leaning forward and cupping Ellie's small chin in one of her hands. 'Don't you see, this is not a bad thing. It's not a disaster. It's a *good* thing!'

'Uh?'

'It's the kick up the fanny-buns we *both* need. It's good medicine.'

It certainly was a kick up the behind. Mind you, she was struggling however to see why they both *needed* it, and why Jez was looking so upbeat about the situation.

'When I picked you up Ellie, you told me you wanted to get the fregg off this cruddy little planet. And so do I. Now, see, the way I look at it….the problem with that job at Dantes was that I was earning *too much*. You and I were getting too damned comfortable sitting on our fat buns, splurging the money away on drink, fancy food templates for our FoodSmart and rinky-dink clothes. It's time to refocus girl. It's time to turn our eyes upwards and *focus*.'

Jez swung an arm around Ellie's shoulders and pushed her forwards so that with a dull thud, her forehead was now pressed up against the scratched plexitex window. Jez pointed outside at the people passing by.

'These fools, these lifeless walking corpses Ellie, are all worried about bills. That's what *they* worry about.'

One of the passers-by, a middle-aged man, haggard and worn down to a stump by the burden of too many years of struggling to make-do in the city, met Jez's gaze. Seeing her finger pointing directly at him, he smiled hopefully, the last of his libido lifting his sallow face into something he must have been hoping approximated a rugged yet attractive smile.

Jez grimaced and flipped the finger back at him.

'Ellie, look up there! Look at the tops of these buildings, the dome and space beyond.'

She obediently looked up, her breath steaming the window so that she had to rub it clear to see. She suddenly realised that raising her eyes like this to gaze up beyond the very tops of the city towers, was something she hadn't done in quite a few days.

'Up there in that big purple sky are the things that the likes of you and I should worry about. Bigger things, better things,' Jez said, staring wistfully up at the faint line of the Veil. 'You can waste time way too easily here,' she added. 'I came in five years ago and I wasn't planning to stop for long. Just enough time to charm my way into enough money to get the fregg out of here.'

Five years ago.

With a chill Ellie realised that one day she too might wake up and realise she had been stuck in the city that long. Probably longer. Too busy pulling every shift available, washing dishes and serving repulsive gunk. Too busy to dream any more. Too busy running just to stand still.

'I propose two things, my diminutive little cube-chik,' Jez announced, settling back on her stool and clasping her hands firmly. 'Firstly, the start of a *two year plan*.'

Ellie drew her eyes away from the darkening night sky. The lights all over New Haven were winking on as the last of the natural light from the world outside slipped away. Advertising holograms began to wink into existence up along the sheer vertical walls of the tenement blocks that towered over and shadowed the narrow street outside.

'Go on,' said Ellie.

'The two year plan is this,' Jez continued. 'We earn as much money as we possibly can. And I mean, we do anything, literally *anything* we can to get that money. And our goal is to have earned enough within two years to buy a ticket - one for each of us - off this shit hole.'

Ellie sat back on her stool and turned to Jez, a look of uncertainty on her face. 'Anything?'

Jez shrugged, 'well almost anything. We don't, you know, sell our bodies or anything like that,' she added curling her lip in disgust at the thought. 'But, we will do anything else. Whatever it takes, okay?'

Despite the fact Ellie was being asked to sign up to a very nebulous plan – the details here were foggy at best - she knew Jez was right. They had been in danger of settling into an almost comfortable rut, becoming part of the cellulite settling on the fat butt of New Haven. With a shudder of guilt, she reminded herself of her promise to Aaron; to not lose sight of her goal to make it off-world. Here she was, she'd *already* done that – thinking of nothing more important than making enough money to keep their cube. To add insult to injury, she had even missed the last two arranged meetings with him. On both occasions, Ellie had realised with a jolt at the last moment that she should have been elsewhere, across the other side of the city with Aaron, instead of shopping with Jez for ever more outrageous accessories. Or slurping Spartans and watching Jez scouting for a sexual partner for the evening.

Oh crap.

Actually, she was loosely scheduled to meet him soon; it was an open repeating invitation; Dionysius, once every two weeks. She just hoped he would bother to turn up again. This time she wasn't going to let him down.

'So?' Jez was looking at her expectantly. 'Whatever it takes Ellie? Right?'

Oh crudge, I'm sorry Aaron.

She was going to damn well make sure she met him. And maybe…just maybe there might be some work he could find for Jez? Manual labour in the port somewhere perhaps? She was strong.

'Ell-eeee? You listening to me?'

Ellie cleared her mind. She smiled. Nodded. 'Okay Jez. Two years…and we'll do whatever the hell it takes.'

Jez's smile widened across her square jaw. 'That's-my-girl,' she said as she leant over and planted a clumsy kiss on her forehead.

Ellie grabbed her sleeve and wiped at the smear of crimson lip-grease above her eyebrows. 'Eewwww, do you have to?'

'And then of course, there's thing number two.'

'Oh yes, thing number two,' Ellie replied warily, remembering that Jez had announced she had two grand proposals to make. She offered a wan smile, not entirely sure what else Jez was going to sign her up to.

'I think we ought to do this to give us a taster of the wild and wonderful universe waiting for us out there, Ellie-girl. Something to kick-start our motivation.'

'I'm not sure I like the sound of this….Do what?'

Jez punched her arm lightly. 'I think you will. I'm going to take you to meet an *alien*.

CHAPTER 6

Jez led Ellie across the city to the seedier end of the Service Sector, where the pavement traffic grew almost too dense to move and the shop and boutique windows came with protective wire-mesh grills.

She kept a firm hold of Ellie's hand as she led the way up a pedestrian ramp away from the crushing soup of humanity towards the foyer of one of the oldest tenement blocks in New Haven. Ellie looked up at the sheer plasteel walls of the gherkin-shaped tower, faded and worn from several decades without proper maintenance. No one lived in the tower any more, except for a few of the more resourceful homeless. Instead, virtually every cube inside the tall phallic building had been illegally occupied by a street vendor. The building awaited demolition. With space at a premium inside the finite domed enclosure of the city, *Baldini Tower* was scheduled to be dismantled and in its place another tenement block erected – one that that stacked living space far more compactly.

Inside the foyer Ellie's senses were assaulted by an over-powering chaos of colours, sounds and odours. It reminded her a little of the trade show; the deafening noise of vendors announcing their wares, special deals, or final offers, and customers and traders haggling.

Jez led her past stall after stall, each one filling a habi-cube with a rich assortment of exotic goods, many of them so full their wares spilled out onto the passageways, arranged haphazardly on boxes and crates. Each ellipsoid doorway was a showcase onto the goods from yet another world she had only ever heard about or seen on the toob. Passing one she was stunned by the rich aroma of spices within; an almost suffocating bouquet of bitter and sweet scents; cinnamotta, quamaric, balusian pepper. They were smells that reminded her of home, of her mother, of family meals together sitting in their messy central dome.

'Baldinis Bizarre Bazaar - this market is a great place to pick up off-world fashions. Here, how about this one?' said Jez as they walked past a stall that stocked a stunning variety of counterfeited fashion garments.

'This is one happy-clappy stall. The best in New Haven. You can pick up any clothes you've seen on the toob, home grown shows, off-world shows…all those clothes, look…'

She pulled a plastex jacket from a rack of them hanging outside the habi-cube door. It was the puffa style jacket that kids in the city seemed to like. She showed Ellie the label.

'*Hardwicker*, a genuine Hardwicker puffa jacket, and what's the price....o-o-only eleven creds. That ain't bad!'

Ellie raised her eyebrows with surprise. She hadn't heard of the label, but clearly it was a big deal if Jez's response was anything to go by.

'Crud, that's cheap. I really, really ought to grab one...but aghh, no! It's too young for me. Baby-girl fashion. Maybe a few years ago, but not...' Jez's voice tailed off as she shuffled briskly through the other jackets.

Ellie spotted a pair of boots that took her fancy. Knee high, a rich, glistening turquoise plastic, with bulging ribbed knee pads that could be folded down inside, or left up, flapping loosely against the knee as one walked. She knelt down and ran her fingers over them.

'Lovely,' she muttered under her breath. She knew Shona would be going totally gaga if she had been here with her right now and could see the range of garments, accessories, trinkets, jewellery, shoes and hats.

'Come on girl,' said Jez grabbing Ellie's shoulder. 'Let's move on. We're here for another reason, not shopping…not this time.'

She grabbed hold of Ellie's hand and dragged her away from the boots, along the passageway towards the ground floor foyer where there was a bank of lifts in the centre of the tower.

They passed a store selling music, movie and toob show clips - all pirate copies naturally. Ellie stopped to watch a holovideo, projecting out into the middle of the passageway of a small bug-eyed character dancing and gyrating to a pounding beat and trilling along to the music with its trademark gibbering catchphrase;

Fibbel-libbel-ring-ding-ding,

oocha coocha eenie feenie, Crazie-Beanie.

'Oh, I love this tune.' She giggled as the computer-generated character performed its track, a catchy ditty Ellie had heard snippets of on the toob over the last few weeks.

Both girls paused, nodded along with the pounding beat, mouthing the meaningless words as if they actually meant something.

'I want to get that tune for my alarm clock,' said Jez. 'It's rinky-dink.'

Ellie nodded. She wasn't up on the music that street kids liked, but she made a special exception for Crazie-Beanie. For some reason the little character made her all but wet herself every time she heard the noises it squeaked and trilled.

Without any warning the holovid was replaced with another; an off-world track that was unfamiliar to either of them.

Jez shrugged. 'Come on.'

Only a few dozen yards further down the passageway they passed by a vendor who had stacked wire cages around his open doorway. Ellie came to a halt, intrigued. She stooped down to look inside one of them. There was something furry in there; something furry and alive.

It was enough of a gesture of curiosity to attract the attention of the tradesman, a slim, darkly grey-skinned man with an oriental slant to his eyes.

'You like them?' he asked.

'I can't see. What is it you've got in there?' she asked. She craned her neck to get a better look inside one of the cages. She could make out several twitching balls of fur, cowering at the far end of the cage, away from her. 'What are those?'

'Podkins,' he replied.

Ellie turned to Jez for a little clarification. 'Podkins?'

'Seed pets,' Jez huffed impatiently. 'You can buy them as seeds, plant them and add water. They grow. You don't need to feed them anything, and they don't poop anywhere. Now can we go please?'

'That's right,' the vendor chipped in, 'no feeding, no pooping. Perfect city pet for the busy town-chik.'

Ellie tapped the cage gently and made a soothing chirruping noise.

'They're so cute.'

She smiled with delight as one of the Podkins pulled itself towards her with one long, furry arm-like protrusion. As it drew closer she could see the small, fist-sized creature seemed to have no face, or any other discernible features.

'Where are its eyes? Mouth?'

The vendor looked at Jez questioningly. And Jez nodded. 'Yeah, she's new to town. You better explain.'

The vendor nodded. 'They have no mouth Miss-chik, because they *don't eat or drink*. You water the little seeds to bring them to life and that's all you need to do. A pet for a month,' said the vendor proudly.

'A month? That's as long as it lives?'

'Ya. Then Miss, it go to *Podkin Heaven*.'

Ellie stuck her bottom lip out in sympathy. 'That's harsh.' A thought occurred to her. 'Is it an alien?'

Jez shook her head. 'No, of course not. Moron. They're engineered. That's right isn't it?' she asked the man.

'Lady is right. A gene-product by Yoki Inc. Engineered to have all the food they ever need right inside them.'

Ellie had a rudimentary knowledge of biology at best, more from watching daytime nature shows on the toob than from anything else. 'So, what, it dies when it runs out of the stored protein inside?'

The vendor waggled his thumb in front of his nose, a gesture Ellie had seen over and over in the city, it was particular to New Haven, and meant something like *nearly*, or *sort of,* or *not quite right.*

'No, not exactly Miss…it dies not because food is gone. It dies because it poison itself with the build up of *shit.*' He shrugged. 'Please excuse…*waste product.*'

Jez shrugged. 'Death by poop. Now there's a really dignified way to go.'

Ellie grimaced. 'That's cruel! If this is an engineered thing…a *designed* thing, why didn't they think to give these poor little critters an…you know?'

'Go on. You can say it Ellie, an *anus*.'

'Well…yes. I mean, crud, every creature deserves at least one.'

The vendor shrugged. 'Would you want to go round and clean up after it, Miss?'

Ellie considered that for a moment. 'I guess not.'

'There! You see? Perfect convenience, perfect design! A little ball of fur that love you with all its heart for a month.' The vendor knelt down beside Ellie and pointed towards the Podkin that had pulled itself across the cage towards her. 'Look, they even design with one little hand so that you have can have something to hold.'

As if responding to the vendors words, the Podkin extended its furry arm and five bald digits, looking disturbingly like the pudgy hand of a newborn baby, reached out towards Ellie. She proffered her index finger through the wire of the cage, gently nudging the pink fleshy folds of the baby-hand. Immediately the fingers wrapped themselves around her reflexively and squeezed her finger with a desperate love – genetically conditioned to do so of course.

'Ideal for the rejected mother,' said Jez dryly. 'Clever design. A cheap baby substitute for those who have had their parental application turned down. That's the kind of monstrosity you get when you let guys in suits design an animal.'

Ellie looked down at the baby hand squeezing her finger. 'It loves you for a month, and then the poor little thing just dies?'

The vendor nodded. 'It take a week to grow full size from the seed,' he replied. 'So, want to buy seeds, Miss? I sell very cheap for you.'

Ellie looked up at Jez. 'Ohhh they are so cute though. What do you think?'

Jez wrinkled her nose. 'If a disembodied baby hand that disappears into a fur ball full of poop does it for you…why not?'

'How much,' Ellie asked.

'Ten, for a packet of five seeds.'

Ellie winced, it was a little too much for her limited budget. 'How about two creds for just one seed?'

The vendor shook his head. 'No, I sell packets of five only…five only.'

Jez sighed impatiently, eager to press on. 'Well look Mister, I'll bet these are counterfeit. They aren't Yoki-gene originals are they? They're engineered locally. Look, two creds for one, or we're walking away.'

The vendor took a moment to consider Jez's offer. 'Three.'

'Come on Ellie, let's go.'

'Okay chik! You taking food from my children's plate. But I go with two.'

'Oh yeah, like you have children,' replied Jez fishing out two creds and handing them over. 'You can square up with me later Ellie-girl.'

The vendor pocketed the money and then handed Ellie what looked like a small pebble.

'This is a Podkin seed, right?' she said looking down at the misshapen black bean in the palm of her hand.

'Of course. You put in some sand, or soil, and water when you get home. That's it.'

Jez tugged impatiently at Ellie. 'Come on you soppy gonk, let's go.'

Ellie looked up at her with a gooey expression on her face. 'Hey, I'm going to be, like, a mum.'

'Mum to a freak furball. Enjoy. Now can we go?'

Ellie nodded.

Jez grabbed Ellie's hand once more and led her down the last of the passageway into a crowded foyer towards the central pillar of lifts.

Only three of the twenty-four lifts still seemed to be functioning. Since the building officially was meant to be unoccupied, no municipal engineers had been sent to repair the systems as one by one they'd broken down. When the last of the lifts failed, the vendors occupying the fifty floors above would probably need to find somewhere else to ply their trade.

They stepped into one of the lifts and Jez punched a button on the wall. A metal grill slid across noisily, with a screech that sounded like a desperate plea for a drop of lube oil.

'So, are we really going to see an alien, Jez? I mean, a real, real one?' she asked as the aging lift carried them jerkily upwards past a dozen blurred floors of colour and chaos.

'Yes, a *real* one. Trust me Ellie. It's a genuine boojam.'

She flushed with excitement. 'Crud, I can't believe it! Where did you hear about it?'

'That dumbass ship loader, remember? The one from the other night?'

Ellie remembered him. Tall, muscular, sopa-dram attractive with tumbling locks of shoulder length dark hair…and as thick as a bowl of lukewarm proto-paste. Exactly Jez's type.

When they reached the twentieth floor, the lift came to a halt with an unsettling clang and the metal grill rolled back. Ellie noticed immediately that things were a lot less busy this high up the tower. Only about half of the cubes had squatting vendors in them, and there were far fewer people ambling down the passageways between.

'And the boojam is up here?'

Jez nodded, 'I'm told so. The ship loader guy said there was one up here plying its trade as a fortune teller.'

Ship-loader guy. Jez didn't even remember his name.

They both proceeded down the corridor, Ellie eyeing the boutiques, noticing that this high up the tower, there were far more black market items and illegal goods on offer than down on the first floor where she'd just bought the Podkin seed. With a chill of recognition she spotted through an open doorway a small arsenal of illegal weapons spread out across a low table. The vendor inside the habi-cube, a pale blue skinned man, with hair gelled up into two stiff glistening devil-horns, met her eyes and then swiftly pulled a rag over them and jerked his head at her to move along.

It made sense that the illegal things, the more risqué items, were on sale up here on the twentieth floor. If any law marshals actually bothered to do their job and paid the tower a visit, there'd be a warning and far more time for those up here to pack away their goods, or perhaps even hurl them down the disposal chutes, than there would be down in the foyer.

'I think that's the one,' said Jez, pointing down the passageway towards a habi-cube doorway on the left. Ellie could see a woman sitting cross-legged outside, draped in swathes of elaborately patterned materials.

As they drew up to the opening she could see around the doorway that someone, presumably this lady, had meticulously painted the same ornate swirling patterns on the plastic walls. It reminded her of some religion she had read about, a religion from Old Earth – *Eslamic*? Something like that. She could smell the rich aroma of burning incense wafting out from the dimly lit cube beyond.

'Hello miss,' said Jez. 'A good friend of mine told me there is a boojam up here, working as a fortune teller.'

The lady smiled pleasantly. Ellie could see she was dark skinned, a sort of dark brown tone. 'Yes. Here in New Haven only for a short time I'm afraid...until His Excellency's work here amongst us is done,' she answered enigmatically.

'Really?' Jez replied with a hint of cynicism. *'His work amongst us*?' she repeated, winking at Ellie. 'So, can we see him? His *Excellency*?'

'Of course you can. Kazan will see anyone who wishes to see him.'

Jez began to step into the darkened cube beyond, but the woman blocked her way with an arm. 'That'll be two credits please, lady.'

'Two credits, huh?

The lady, still smiling, nodded. 'Of course. Kazan has to eat just like anyone else.'

Ellie leaned forward. 'Is that two credits each? Or for the pair of us?'

The woman stared up at her and reached out a hand towards Ellie. She grabbed one of her hands and stroked it gently. 'So young, you are. Just a child. Why are you here? This city is no place for a young boy.'

'I'm not a boy!' replied Ellie, a little piqued. She pulled her hand back. 'I'm not a child either!'

'Please forgive.' The woman studied her carefully. 'Far, far older than your years I think.' She nodded towards the entrance to the darkened habi-cube beside her. 'For you then, *lady*….you have a good strong karma. I let you both in for three credits. Three, the pair of you.'

'Thank you,' said Jez. 'Come on, Ellie.'

Ellie was somewhat baffled by the woman's words.

'You ready then Ellie? Your first alien?'

She forgot the woman's esoteric nonsense about karmas. She nodded. An excited grin spread across her lips. All of a sudden here it was, she was about to do one of the things she had told Sean that she hoped she one day would; to finally meet a real alien. The growing excitement of the moment stole the reply from her mouth.

'Then let's go do it, girl,' said Jez, dragging her friend in through the open door.

CHAPTER 7

Inside the cube the ever present neon-lights of New Haven night-time had been blocked out with more elaborate patterned materials draped over the two round windows. Ellie looked around the small cube. Once upon a time this had been someone's living space. Stains and marks on the fibre-mat floor told a brief tale of long gone tenants, and long ago spills and mishaps. The modest oval room was illuminated by half a dozen candles burning steadily on a low table in front of a hooded figure, which sat on a pile of scattered cushions on the floor.

'Uh...hello. *Kazan*, is it?' whispered Jez, a little self-consciously. 'We've come to have our fortunes told.'

The hooded figure stirred slightly, then after a moment of stillness, an arm emerged from within the voluminous robes and gestured to some cushions in front of the table. Ellie caught a glimpse of the boojam's skin. By the candle-light it looked pale, densely textured and contoured with wrinkles, like very old suede or leather. The

71

arm ended with an odd hand; two equally long and thick digits splayed like a 'Y'.

'You coming in, and sitting here,' Kazan said, his voice rustled like dry leaves caught by a breeze. To Ellie, the asthmatic rustling and whispering behind the words reminded her of restless and hungry tubweeds stirring impatiently.

'Thank you,' she replied, taking a seat on the floor in front of the low table. Jez sat down beside her.

'For three creds you'd think they could afford chairs,' Jez muttered. Ellie shushed her.

Kazam's hood twitched oddly and they both heard a sniffing sound coming from within the darkened folds. All of a sudden, a pale tentacle-like shape emerged from the hood, from where Ellie assumed the creature's face must be. The pale tentacle arced upwards and towards both girls like a strange headless cobra rearing up in readiness to strike at them. Ellie pulled back nervously and grabbed her friend's hand.

'Hey, relax,' said Jez calmly, 'it's all part of the show.'

The tentacle probed the air then, after a moment of hesitation, it drifted towards Jez, holding a position several inches in front of her face; two bulbous glands surrounded by wrinkles of loose skin, a small moist hole between the glands that puckered and flexed. It wafted gently to and fro as it delicately sampled the air around her.

Jez giggled. 'It looks like a man's dingy-thingy.'

'Uh?'

'You know, a guy-handle? A meat joystick.'

'Eww.' Ellie wrinkled her face in disgust. 'They look like that?'

'Seriously?' Jez looked at her. 'You've never got this close to a-'

'You am wanting future, tell?' The dry whispering voice came from beneath the hood. Impatient.

'Oh, sorry. Yes, we do!' Jez replied. 'My friend, Ellie here, and I....well we have a plan. We want to-'

Ellie grasped Jez's arm. 'See if he can guess what our plan is first,' she whispered.

Jez paused for a moment. 'Good idea,' she replied quietly. 'Okay, see...we've got something we both want to do, Mr Kazan. Can you guess what it is?'

Kazan's body wobbled under his cloak and they heard what sounded like laughter. 'What goal you am wish to do?'

Both girls nodded, 'yes.'

'Like me, of course…am wishing leave planet,' he replied. 'Too tired of here, am wishing to go.'

Ellie looked at Jez and squeezed her hand with excitement. 'Wow. He guessed! That's incredible!'

'Aw freg. That's a pretty easy guess, Ellie.' Jez replied quietly, as the boojam's trunk-like nose continued to hover inches away from her face. 'That was too easy.'

Kazam's form wobbled again. 'Yes. Is far too easy. Planet sucks.'

The girls looked at each other and giggled.

'Now, you want I to read future path you am taking?'

Both of them nodded. 'Yeah,' they chorused enthusiastically.

The boojam inhaled deeply, his body expanding under the cloak as they heard the air whistling into twin slits at the end of his trunk.

'Ahhhhh,' Kazan exhaled after a moment and the air he had sucked in blew back out of the trunk into Jez's face. She grimaced at the rancid smell coming back at her. 'You lady, sense you strong…strong as many.

You am lived long time here, now time comes soon when you am planning to leave.'

The mirth on Jez's face began to vanish with the mysterious, hypnotic rustling of his voice. She was entranced by the gently swinging trunk in front of her.

'So tell me, I'm going to get off Harpers Reach, right?'

'Time will come soon, two possibilities, two branches. One branch, you leave. The other....you not,' the boojam replied.

'Crud. How soon does this branch thingy happen then? Are we talking weeks? Months? Years?'

'Sooner than you think,' the alien replied. 'Am smell things already in motion, you...moved by them.'

'Do I get to pick the right branch then? Come on...tell me, do I get off this crud-hole?'

The boojam hesitated, 'the answer exist inside you, listen to it.'

Jez looked confused for a moment, her eyebrows furrowed in concentration. 'I'm listening, not hearing anything though.'

'What you wish to hear?'

'That I get the freg off this world.'

The boojam hesitated again. Ellie wondered if it was deciding whether to tell

Jez what she wanted to hear. *The paying customer is always right.*

'That…is the answer.'

'Yes!' hissed Jez. She turned to Ellie and nudged her arm. 'Tell me, Kazam, what will I see out there in space? Will I meet some rich young stud and party for the rest of my life?' Jez asked, grinning expectantly.

Kazan's trunk lifted up from her face and hovered in the air above her head. Again they heard the boojam inhale deeply and the whistle of air entering his trunk. He held it in for a few moments before exhaling again.

'Uncertainty in life. Long or short. Unsure,' he answered. 'But destiny is not yours. You destiny am tied to things other, bigger.'

'Okay, I'm happy with that,' she answered. 'Die young or old, at least it looks like I'm finally going to get off this mud ball. See, Ellie? It's our destiny to get out of here.'

Kazan's trunk gently tapped against her head as he hissed. 'Now be quiet'.

It swung across and curled towards Ellie. She found herself flinching uncertainly as the pale, wrinkled end of it wavered only inches away from her face. Her eyes were drawn to the two narrow orifices on the end;

slits of flesh that opened, puckered and closed like tiny mouths sipping the air.

'Now, you,' said Kazan. Both orifices suddenly flared, opening widely as Ellie felt a draft of air being sucked in, brush across her cheeks. She found herself struggling to hold onto a nervous giggle.

Nerves. Or perhaps it was the preposterous nature of their fortune-teller. Ellie had never before heard of one's fortune being *smelled*. She bit her lip to stop her chuckling out loud as the boojam held the air in his lungs and began sampling the unique cocktail of chemicals that was supposedly an indication of her future.

'If I'd known we were coming out to have our fortunes read, I might have had a shower first,' whispered Ellie uncomfortably as they waited in silence. Jez snorted.

'Quiet!' Kazan snapped, his rustling, whispering voice momentarily a loud bark.

Jez closed her mouth and clamped her lips tightly together. She did her best to maintain a demeanour of solemnity. Her jiggling shoulders were all that gave her away. Ellie kept her eyes firmly on the boojam's trunk, knowing full well that right now - keyed up with excitement as she was - catching sight of Jez would set her off.

At last the alien exhaled again and she felt a warm blast of fetid air across her cheeks.

'You future complicated. Am difficult to read. Much things in there.'

Ellie's urge to giggle was kicked to the side for the moment. She leant to one side to look at the robed figure. 'Do I get off of this world too?' she asked impatiently. 'That's the one thing I really want to know. Please.'

'Yes. You leaving, am going far, far away this world. See many worlds.'

Ellie clasped her hands together with sheer unbridled delight. 'Oh-my-crud! I'm getting off!?' she cried. 'Tell me, when. How soon?'

Kazan nodded. 'Soon. But...' he raised one of his two-digit hands. 'Other things am seeing. Uncertain...you. Am seeing, many death, war.....change, rebirth,' the boojam whispered, its rustling voice increasing in volume.

'Woah, Ellie! This is getting interesting,' whispered Jez, the grin fading from her face too.

'Many changes, you at the centre....changes radiating out, like a star.'

Suddenly Kazan twitched violently and with one of his hands the boojam threw his hood back to reveal his face. The skin was pallid and wrinkled like his arms. Above where the trunk emerged from his face, Ellie saw a cluster of four or five small, watery, beady black eyes, like a bunch of grapes, studying her intensely. Either side of his face, large fanned ears flickered and stretched out like small wings. Ellie lurched backwards as the boojam suddenly leant towards her.

'One *seeks* you! One hunts you! You destiny decided by which find you first,' he growled loudly.

'Uh?'

The trunk recoiled from Ellie, curled back towards his face. 'You must leave this world quickly! Leave now!'

The woman who had taken their money at the door bustled in, disturbed by the boojam's raised voice. 'Everything all right, Kazam?'

The boojam was quivering within his robes, the trunk flailing agitatedly from side to side.

'What did you two do to him?!'

'Nothing,' said Jez. 'He just went all weird.'

'Please, you must go now. You can see he is upset. He never shows his face like this! Never!'

'Achh! Am see dying in someone close to you!' the boojam continued, voice raised, shrill, almost feminine. 'War! Death!'

'Out!' cried the woman. 'Now!'

The girls got to their feet awkwardly under the stern gaze of the woman, but Kazan reached out with one of his hands and grabbed Ellie's arm. His skin felt surprisingly soft and warm, and despite its unattractive pallor and the wrinkles, she felt the alien's grasp comforting, reassuring even.

'Must leave from this world, as soon as can. Understanding? Waste no time!'

Ellie nodded silently. 'That's what we're trying to-'

'Please, you girls, leave now! You've upset him, can't you see?' the woman said, pulling at Ellie's arm.

*

It wasn't until they had walked out of the old Baldini Tower and grabbed a skyhound heading back to their part of the city that Jez finally broke the thoughtful silence.

'Well...um....actually that was *supposed* to be a bit of a laugh.'

Ellie nodded, she was still pondering the confusing things the alien had told her.

'People are after me?' she said looking at Jez. 'What have I done to anyone?'

'Fregg, I don't know, girl. Maybe he was talking about your farm folks. Maybe he was just fancying it up a bit to make it sound good. You know, messing with your mind. But, I'll say this for free - he was right about one thing; the sooner we get a wriggle on and get out of New Haven, the better.'

'Yeah,' Ellie replied distractedly, Kazan's cryptic warnings still tumbling around in her head.

'So, smelly Ellie,' Jez's face brightened. 'When we get back it's your turn to program dinner. And then we sit down and we start thinking how we'll get enough money to find a way off. Okay?'

'Okay.'

'I don't think your job at that cruddy diner is going to get you anywhere in a hurry, so….we *both* need to get out there and find ourselves better jobs.'

'And how are we going to do that, Jez?' she asked, staring out of the window at the bustling city below. 'There's like two million other people out there ragging for jobs, just like us. Just 'cause we want decent jobs, doesn't mean we'll find any.'

Jez nodded. 'True, but then there's one huge thing in our favour.'

'What's that?'

'They're all butt-ugly,' she grinned.

'Oh right, yeah,' shrugged Ellie, 'that's just great Jez. That might work for you. But I'm not exactly a toob-face.'

'Look at them,' she said gesturing to the passengers around them in the hound. 'All of them...miserable, grey-faced, brain-dead ditto-drekks!'

Ellie was relieved that most, if not all of them, were wearing earphones and watching either hand-held toob sets or the holovid image projected onto one of the plasti-screen windows. She did notice one middle-aged woman scowling indignantly back at them. Ellie smiled apologetically. 'Sorry, she doesn't really know what she's say-'

'Now,' Jez continued, 'take you and I, we both look great.'

Ellie looked at her with raised eyebrows. 'What?'

'Alright, I... look great. With a bit of work, you look passable. But, together, if we smile enough, we make a winning combo. We've just got to think *big,* girl. Think Big...and smile lots.'

'And you think it's going to be that easy?' she replied looking back out of the window once more. 'Smile a lot and bat our eyelids?'

'That's what Madge Muggerzink says in Shuttle Stop 9, isn't it? *Think Big, Smile Lots and the world is your Soyo-Snack.*'

'Oh, right. It must be true then.'

Jez pinched Ellie's nose and pulled her round to look into her eyes. 'Have I led you wrong yet?'

'Nobe Jez, I guebb you haben't,' she replied sullenly.

OMNIPEDIA:
[Human Universe digital encyclopaedia]

Article: Ellie Quin > Terraforming

The beginning of the thirty-fifth century saw the re-emergence of the 21st century disease; Parasitic Corporatism. Looking back with the clear vision of hindsight, it is obvious that by Ellie Quin's time, behind the velvet glove of the Colonial Administration, the real power lay with large system-wide business interests. Studying this fascinating period of history, their steady influence on the Administration's governance of Human Space is almost impossible to ignore. However, at the time, although it was apparent to those few who chose to open their eyes and see it, for the vast majority of human citizens the omnipresence of only a few dozen corporations in every city, on every planet, must have been an acceptable norm.

History has shown us again and again, that when the value of an endeavour is measured solely in profit, something will *always* go wrong. The best example of this principle was the terraforming industry. This was dominated by only a handful of corporations competing aggressively for contracts, and rushing the delicate processes of atmosphere conversion to reduce their operating costs. The cataclysmic mismanagement of Celestion's atmosphere was perhaps one of the more notorious examples of this. Over half a million people died on the planet because the company, Hale-Hale Worlds, attempted to halve the projected time span of the process....all in the name of profit.

User Comment > Yoki-Industries
Want a career in Terraforming? Join WorldFast: the fastest growing provider of planet-wide solutions. For more information quote 'WorldFast > jobs'

User Comment > Phil-100232
It's no better now than it was back then. Mega-companies own Human Space. Everyone knowz that, don't they?

CHAPTER 8

'Hi Hufty, it's been a while again. I really must record my diary more often. Well, where do I start? Things have changed a bit since the last time I did some diary. Jez lost her job dancing at that night club, but…she decided that it was for the best. It's made her think about what she wants to do with her life and she's really set her mind now on getting off Harpers Reach. So, being the bossy loud-chik that she is, she made me quit my job at the slap 'n' grill….it was a daggy job anyway….so we could both *upsize our income* together. I think that's the phrase she used.'

'In a way I'm sort of pleased that that happened; Jez losing her dancing job. I think she would have stayed there forever otherwise, and she deserves better than that. Anyway, it's good, because now we've both decided to work towards the one goal together. We've made a pact….a deal sort of. Well, it's more like a mantra; '*Off-world or die trying.*' What do you think? Catchy, huh?'

'Oh yeah...I called home and spoke to Dad again. He's still hopping mad with me, but not as bad as the last time I spoke to him. I told him I had somewhere to live, a good friend and some work to keep me busy. He made me promise to visit soon, which, you know, I'd like to do, I really would. I miss them all so much, but it's more than I can afford right now. A shuttle flight back home would be like, I guess....it would take me a year to earn that much. Anyway, if I can save a bit every month? Well, we'll see.'

'Dad told me, he's starting to change over the crop now. He's taken the tubweed out of Betsy and changed the filters and climate control. That's the good news. The bad news is that it's going to be pretty gross getting things right with the meat crop he's trying out. They're so hard to keep alive. Yeuuchh! He says Sean's Dad is going to help set it up for him, get it right so they don't end up with the mess they had the first time he tried.'

'Speaking of Sean, I wonder how he is? I guess the Freezer must have taken him back to that army planet and they must be all defrosted now and doing their training. I asked Dad if Sean had sent anything yet, but he said there'd been nothing so far. I hope he writes. You know, I miss him too. I know he's out there, he's seen space for himself....I wish I could see what he must be seeing. I'd love to tell him I've seen an alien. I wonder if *he* has yet? Crud! I wish Sean would write to me; give me an address so I can tell him everything that's happened to me. I know he would be super-impressed. I know he would.'

'Oh well Hufty, I've got to go now. Jez's shouting to me to get a move on. We've both got an interview at this fast food place, 'StarBreaks'. The creds are good there, and it'll mean we'll be working together. Which will be nice. I think.'

*

'So, what makes you the right girls for the job then?' asked Mr Noah. He leant backwards in his chair, studying them carefully as they both looked at each other.

'Well,' Jez started, 'we're both hardworking chiks. We really are....and dedicated to any job that we take on, dedicated, and fiercely loyal of course,' she continued.

Ellie studied Noah, and realised looking at him, and then casting a glance over his rounded shoulder at the other staff, busy serving a lunchtime crowd, that she knew the answer he was after.

'Because we look pretty normal, right?'

Jez cocked an eyebrow. But Noah nodded slightly.

'Quite right.'

Ellie had noticed that coming into the city; so many of its inhabitants seemed to be genetically *varied* in some way. Mostly, what differed were the skin colours. She had seen so many *natural* colours ranging from a zombie-like white, to an almost lemon yellow or a bright citrus-orange…to the darkest midnight black. That kind of diversity was mostly a result of engineering; skin hues toned to best suit the rays of the varied stars in Human Space. There were, of course, many other noticeable traits she had noticed; people hairier than normal, taller, thinner, thickset, lean. A well known characteristic of citizens from much larger planets was that they were engineered to be shorter and more muscular in order that their bodies could cope better with a higher gravity environment. It was no secret that the Administration made sure that babies were best suited to the worlds they were destined to live on. Common sense really. What it did mean was that on a world like

Harpers Reach that seemed to attract drifters from other worlds, it made for an interesting mix of genetically modified people.

But there was something else she had noticed, mostly from watching the toob. There was a perceived *norm*, a preferred look, that *most,* if not *all,* the celebrities and presenters on the toob conformed to. The look was referred to as 'gene-neutral'.

Looking at Noah and his staff, she could tell he preferred his workforce to look as gene-neutral as possible. Not too fat or thin, not too tall or short, not too orange or yellow or black; not too far off the 'normal' coffee-to-cream skin colours that most people were used to seeing on every advertising holoscreen in the city.

Gene Neutral.

'Yes,' he added. 'No place in StarBreaks for some of the odd-looking drekks out there. No one likes a freak handling their food for them. Not even another freak, I can tell you.'

Jez nodded. 'Yeah, well no way we're freaks, Mr Noah.'

Ellie noticed something else too. No male staff, or at least none that she could see right now.

'And they got to look *nice* too,' added Mr Noah. 'No one wants their StarMeal handed to them by somebody with a hair-lip, or a mono-brow, or spots or dry skin. *Nice* looking people, if you know what I mean,' he said. His eyes travelled quickly over Ellie's narrow frame, and lingered long and lecherously on Jez's more pronounced contours.

'It's a busy StarBreaks here, one of the top five outlets in New Haven,' said Noah cracking his large knuckles. 'I hire only the best girls here. The best looking and the hardest working.'

Noah stood up, his wide frame jiggling beneath his loose-fitting shirt. He pointed through his plexiglaz office door at the bustling activity outside. The twenty-foot long service counter was manned by half a dozen young girls, many of whom, Ellie guessed, were probably young farm girls like her.

She noticed they were all far prettier too.

'People come here for their StarFagurter because they get served quicker than anywhere else, and they get a pretty smile free with the food. I don't do Happy Meals, or novelty plastic toys, or two-for-one promotions. I don't need to. My StarGirls bring the customers in,' he said continuing to address them - Jez in particular. 'So that's the blah-blah-blah bit. Now here's the deal; I pay six and a half creds an hour. You want the job?'

Jez turned to Ellie and shrugged her shoulders. 'Actually, that's not bad,' she muttered.

'Uh....I'm afraid the offer's only for you,' said Noah to Jez.

Jez shook her head. 'That case, no. We come as a pair Mr Noah. If there's no job for Ellie too, then I'm not interested.'

'Plus,' he added quickly, 'you get to keep one percent of your till takings. The more you convince them to up-size, the more you take home.'

Jez did a double-take. 'You do a commission on top of the pay?'

Noah nodded, 'you notice all my girls are smiling out there?

'That's pretty good money, Ellie.' Jez said. She squirmed with guilt as she considered the offer for a moment.

'Crud! Jez, take the job. I'll find something else easily,' Ellie replied forcing a wan smile. 'You should go for it.'

Jez pursed her lips while she wrestled with the dilemma. *She* had encouraged Ellie to chuck in her last job. It had been *her* Big Idea for them to both go hunting for work together, offering their services as a team. She felt responsible for Ellie, especially now she didn't have any job at all. But then, the money here seemed pretty damned good. Jez knew she could effortlessly flirt her way to making customers double up their orders; earning a nice helping of till commission on top of what was a pretty decent pay package.

Dilemma-dilemma-dilemma....

Finally she turned back to him. 'No, it's both of us or nothing doing, Mr Noah.'

Noah put his hands on his wide hips and clucked and whistled whilst he studied both of the girls. His eyes darted from Jez to Ellie, and then back again. Ellie found herself subconsciously straightening her back, thrusting her slight chest forward and pouting her thin lips ever so slightly at Noah. Hating herself for doing that and then slumping back in the chair. She gave up. She knew she couldn't do that flirty kind of thing as well as Jez.

'Are you a smart kid?' he asked Ellie.

'Yes, I think so.'

'You pick things up quick?'

Ellie nodded, 'sure.'

'And you're a hard worker?'

'Yes, a very, very hard worker, Mr Noah.'

He shook his head and smiled wearily. 'Okay, I'll take you both on. But you,' he said pointing at Ellie, 'I think I'll put you on the call-ins cubicle.'

She sighed with relief, pleased that she wouldn't be walking away on her own, still looking for a job out there without Jez beside her.

'Yeah, you can take the call-in orders. Think you can do that chik?'

'Yes sir, I'm sure I can,' Ellie answered cheerfully.

'Of course you can. It's not rocket science.' Noah gestured for them both to stand up. 'Alright then, interview's over. Tomorrow morning at seven sharp, I want you here, and in uniform.'

The door slid open with a soft swish, and the chaotic noise of the service counter outside flooded in. He reached down towards a locker and pulled out two bundles of shrink-wrapped clothes, each bearing a large golden 'S'.

'Your uniforms,' he said, 'come wearing them tomorrow morning.'

Ellie and Jez headed out of the door. Noah lightly patted Jez on her butt as she passed by. 'See you at seven, don't be late,' he said with a wink. Jez gritted her teeth as she followed Ellie from the StarBreaks fast food restaurant onto the pedestrian walkway outside.

'Ugghh. What a complete slime ball,' she said pulling a face.

'We got the jobs! We're working together!'

Jez smiled. 'What did I tell you? Think Big, Smile Lots.'

They wandered to the edge of the walkway and Ellie leant against the guard rail, looking down at the churning city below. They were on one of the highest pedestrian zones in the city, a plaza of shops and eateries that filled the empty space between three large, closely clustered towers. 'It's an amazing view from up here.'

'Yeah, doobie view,' replied Jez distracted, studying the shrink wrapped package in her hands suspiciously.

'Let's see then,' said Ellie as she tore open her package and pulled out the uniform. It was a pair of navy blue trousers and a sky-blue shirt, the yellow 'S' proudly displayed on two breast pockets, and the collar.

'Hey, that's not so bad,' she said hesitantly. 'Could have been worse, I guess.'

Jez looked back at hers with a wary expression as she opened her package. She pulled out a navy blue ultra-mini skirt, that was clearly barely going to cover her crotch and a skin-hugging sky blue lycra top. She studied them with disgust.

'Oh, please,' she said. 'These are so cheesy.'

'What's that?' said Ellie pointing at something else in the package. Jez looked down and pulled out the final item of the StarBreak uniform; navy blue knickers with a fluffy white pompom on the rear.

'Oh for fregg's sake,' she muttered holding the garment up in one hand and staring at it with disgust. 'I didn't notice any of the counter staff wearing these.'

Ellie cast her mind back and recalled a flash of white as one of the girls behind the counter had bent over, almost double, to pull out a tray and sauce cartons from a low shelf *facing* the service counter. No doubt a contrived design of the restaurant's layout to ensure a teasing glimpse of white bunny-tail for the waiting customer.

A sky car roared past, momentarily bathing them both in its brilliant headlight beams.

'Oh well,' Ellie patted Jez on the shoulder, 'just think of the money. All that extra commission a good-looking girl like you can earn.'

Jez nodded. 'It's not the ogling from losers like that I mind,' she nodded towards the queue of customers leading out through the restaurant's doorway onto the plaza. They were mostly male, of course, standing silently in line as they waited for their fast food lunch. 'I'm used to seeing their kind at Dantes. I can handle a bit of eye-fondling Ellie-girl. It's this cheesy-peasy uniform, I'm gonna' have a problem coping with. That and Mr Noah undressing me every time he looks at me.'

Ellie smiled sympathetically. 'We don't have to take this job. I'm sure there are others.'

'Crud...let's give it a go. The money sounds good enough. And we've got ourselves a goal now anyway. The sooner we can buy our way off of this poo-stack the better.'

Ellie couldn't have agreed more, although she wasn't the one that was going to have to wear the bunny tail knickers.

CHAPTER 9

'So that's one Star Fagurter, one Star Chopper-double-proto-slab with a side of synthicheese, two orders of StarRings and a couple of StarMega-gloops?'

'Yeah,' the young man replied lethargically over the holo-vid display.

'That'll be ten creds, point fifty-five, please,' said Ellie. She looked up at the dummy-card on the wall beside her in the booth. 'Oh yeah, if your order goes over fifteen creds, you get the twenty minute delivery promise,' she added with a smile and a well deployed tone of infectious enthusiasm.

'Yeah? What's that then?'

'Oh? The promise? You get it within twenty minutes, otherwise you pay absolutely nothing.'

The man on the end of the call shrugged casually. 'Oh, Right. Stick another couple of side orders of rings on then.'

'*Star*Rings, sir?' Ellie said, remembering Mr Noah's dictum that if it wasn't *Star*-food it wasn't on the menu.

'Rings?, *Star*Rings?...whatever, chik. Just stick another two orders on. What's that make it now?'

Ellie kept her till-smile firmly in place, as she added the side-orders to the rest and checked the total. 'Fifteen credits and ten, sir,' she beamed cheerfully back at him.

'Fine.' The man swiped at something out of sight and the till instantly registered the payment.

'Your order will be there in twenty minutes or less. Thank you for eating with-'

'Whatever,' the man replied before disconnecting the call.

Charming.

Ellie looked up at the delivery roster display and saw the order appear on the end of the list, and alongside it the timer displayed nineteen minutes and fifty-nine seconds left. Already valuable seconds were ticking away. The previously placed orders in the queue were busy counting down too and already dispatched and on their way through the humming airspace of New Haven on the back of a delivery d-ped.

'Despatch order 997, another with the twenty minute promise,' said Ellie into her throat mic, knowing that almost immediately, one of the delivery-girls would be hopping on a d-ped, gunning the engine and anxiously waiting for the order to slide through and be placed into the warm-box on the back.

Noah stuck his head into the order cubicle and looked at the delivery roster display. 'Everything all pukkadoo?'

Ellie nodded. 'Yes Mr Noah.'

'Good, you're selling the delivery deal?'

'Yes, sir. Every order so far has been over fifteen creds.'

Noah reached out a large flabby hand and ruffled her hair. 'Atta-girl,' he said. 'None of those suckers out there actually bother to clock the time the order takes anyway. Good girl,' he muttered as he closed the door of the cubicle again.

Ellie patted down her messed-up hair and smiled with a vague sense of satisfaction. Four days on the job and already she felt like she had it pretty much nailed. Mr Noah seemed satisfied with the way things were going. Okay so she might not be a big crowd-puller on the counter, but she was doing an efficient job taking the orders, she hadn't made a single mistake yet.

The call-order cubicle was a solitary plexitex blister on the side of the StarBreaks building that overhung the edge of the pedestrian plaza. As she waited for the next order, she cast a glance downwards past her feet, through the plastic bubble to the city below. The first morning she had settled into the cubicle she had suffered a terrible, dizzying bout of vertigo as she studied the tiny dark dots of milling people on the ground far below, and the larger swooping blurs of airborne traffic passing by beneath her. But now she had grown accustomed to it, it was a spectacular distraction to fill the few slack moments in the day between taking and despatching orders.

*

Jez looked the two young boys firmly in the eyes. They were perhaps only a year younger than Ellie. Scruffy young street-shavs, both of them grinning, showing gemstone teeth implants and countless pigment-swirl arm tattoos.

And they were also taking the piss.

'I already gave you some StarSauce cartons,' she replied icily pointing to the tray. 'There? See them?'

The bigger of the two young lads, winked at her. 'Well, I'd like another, miss.'

Jez turned round reluctantly and bent down to grab another few cartons from the dispenser. As she did, she heard both of the young boys snigger.

'Hey *Star*Chik, nice tail.'

She gritted her teeth as she stood up again and slapped the sauce cartons down on the tray along with the other ones they had already asked for.

Just keep your cool, girl. She dug down deep and pulled out her best over-the-counter-smile. 'Is that everything?' she said flatly through her teeth.

The tallest of the two young boys leaned casually against the counter taking his best shot at appearing sophisticated and cool. 'So, you got a tug-friend? You want to go love-pup with me, chik? One-on-one date-action?' he asked, his adolescent voice warbling up and down awkwardly along with his bobbing Adam's apple.

She sighed.

Although this StarBreaks outlet turned out to be conveniently close to home, it seemed unfortunately, to also be one of the principle gathering points for New Haven's young bucks. More specifically, the young lads who skulked around in the daylight hours in their hooded puffas, and at night raised a racket surfing the various tower's thermals on their carbolite-boards.

'Sorry…I'm betrothed,' she replied drily, 'anything else?'

'Uh?'

'Anything else?'

'That's it.' He turned to his friend and flicked his wrist.

She took the boy's money and then turned to the auto-chef and voiced-in the order. As she waited for the StarMeal to be restructured on the other side behind the fascia of the machine from raw blobs of protein paste, she looked across the kitchen to the order cubicle. She saw Ellie taking another call-in. Her friend looked up and they shared a grin and a wave.

'Hey! Chik!'

Jez cursed quietly and slowly turned round to face the boy. 'How about my mate?' he said, pointing to the kid standing beside him, who, despite the off-world scarlet hue of his skin, had managed to go a tone more red.

Jez ground her teeth. The cheeky little jerk was a determined little sod. She leant forward across the counter. 'Not in a million years,' she muttered under her breath, 'not if either of you dick squirts were the last pulse on this planet.'

There was a soft ping from behind her and, with a sense of relief, she turned round, picked the steaming-hot meal up, placed it on the tray and pushed the tray across the counter.

'Thank you,' she said with hooded eyes and her lips turned up into a sneer. The boy turned away with a victorious smirk on his face, no doubt convinced by some nuance in her reply that he had successfully arranged some sordid little group activity for her with him and his friend.

Jez continued to grind her teeth as she watched the boys swagger outside to join several of their friends, hanging around the entrance to the restaurant in a surly group. She watched the jerk who had placed the order tell his tale of conquest, pointing in her direction once briefly, and then watched them as they laughed and cast several furtive glances her way.

If she wasn't wearing this bloody degrading uniform and on StarBreak hours, she could quite happily go out there and knock a few of their little coconut heads together.

Think of the money girl.

She prepared her composure for the next customer in line; a scruffy looking old man who smiled with a lecherous twinkle in his eyes.

She mustered her best Miss Cheerful singsong voice.

'Good morning, how can I help you sir?'

'Can I have some more sauce, please, love.'

*

Their lunch break was mid-afternoon, after the usual midday torrent had settled down to a steady trickle of business. The restaurant was just ticking over with one or two of the counter staff still serving whilst the rest of the girls hurried out to enjoy their twenty minute break.

Ellie and Jez wandered across the plaza and found a street vendor selling coffee and meatie-flasties. They sat down on a bench towards the edge of the plaza to enjoy a view of the hazy city as they ate their lunch. The sinking afternoon sun from the baking clay-orange world outside, cast a strong peach hue through the foggy dome and across the shimmering urban skyline. Every now and then, the flash of reflected sunlight off the hood of an aircar, or the metallic flanks of a skyhound.

'I'm really not sure I can do this counter job,' said Jez after her first bite.

Ellie wasn't entirely surprised. Every now and then, when things were a little less busy she had been checking to see how Jez was doing. And it seemed every time she had looked across, Jez had her back to the counter, was scowling furiously and was muttering something under her breath.

'I'm used to being ogled at. I can handle that, Ellie. It's just this stupid daggy pompom that's really getting under my skin. I feel like a complete cret'.' Jez turned to her. 'You know how I look is important to me, don't you?'

Ellie nodded. 'I know.' Jez was singularly the vainest person she had ever met in her short life.

'Did you know, they don't wear this kind of crud at any of the other StarBreaks? Did you know that?'

Ellie shook her head, 'I thought that was standard counter uniform.'

'Yeah, well, what *you're* wearing is. But the skirt thing and the pompom thing is Noah's big idea. Dirty old sod. It's…it's…' Jez took another bite out of her meatie-flasty, barely tasting the soyo-tang filling.

'Demeaning?' offered Ellie.

Jez's eyebrows furrowed, 'if that means it makes me look like a complete idiot, then yes.'

They watched a skyhound approach the plaza and then disgorge several dozen people onto a bubble-stop nearby, before sailing gracefully down to join a traffic stream below them.

'I'm going to ask Noah if he can move me to some other job. It's those shavs that gather outside; those cocky young boys that get under my skin the most. Little…little runts think they can hit on me, just because I'm dressed like a fregging bunny rabbit.'

'Well, you could see if Noah will let you work in deliveries. You know they get paid a commission per delivery, so the more you can deliver, the more you'll get.'

Jez nodded unenthusiastically. 'Yeah, I suppose I could.'

'And you get to wear the normal version of the uniform.'

'Bonus,' replied Jez.

Ellie thought about it some more. 'Actually, I could cherry-pick your orders.'

'What do you mean?'

'Give you orders grouped closely together…so that you can take more than one at a time. You know this part of the city like the back of your hand, right?'

'Yeah.'

'You know all the shortcuts. We could really stack your deliveries. I'll give you all the ones in the same area, and you could do two or three customers with each run. I think it's like a cred per delivered order that Noah pays out in delivery bonus. You could be earning two or three creds every twenty minutes, that's another nine creds per hour.'

Jez sat upright and stared at her. 'On top of my basic pay….that's…that's-'

'Fifteen and a half per hour,' replied Ellie. 'Not bad, uh?'

'Ellie-girl, ' Jez said, grasping her narrow shoulders with both hands. 'You may not be a cutie-chik, but you are most definitely the brains of our little team. Crud…I'm going back right now to talk to that big lump, Mr Noah. He's going to transfer me, girl. Or I'll pull his stubby little nose off and serve it up with the next order.'

Jez finished her meatie, and swigged the last few gritty mouthfuls of coffee before turning and striding defiantly back across the busy plaza towards StarBreaks. She pushed her way nonchalantly through an idling crowd of offworlders, several of

108

whom wolf-whistled her as they watched her bunny tail swing with each angry stride.

Ellie watched her go and smiled with admiration at Jez's natural, antagonistic, self confidence. She envied that quality of hers more than anything else. Only someone like Jez could casually push her way through a pack of rough-looking men like those, dressed the way she was, without a single shred of humility. If Ellie could exchange one characteristic with Jez, it wouldn't be her beautiful, some might say, striking face, nor her curvaceous frame, nor the husky tom-boy voice that men seemed to find so attractive; it would be none of those things.

It would be that ability of hers to effortlessly front-out everything.

She seemed to have an air of assurance that made her appear almost invincible. Nothing or no-one was ever going to best Jez. She wore confidence like an impenetrable force field.

CHAPTER 10

Jez breezed into Noah's office without knocking. 'I need a word,' she announced sternly.

Noah glanced up from his data screen, a look of irritation spread across his face. 'I'd like you to go outside, knock, and then try again.'

Jez ignored him. The door swished closed behind her and she took several intimidating steps forward. 'I want a transfer *off* the counter.'

'What?' he uttered, thrown off balance momentarily. Noah recovered his composure quickly and offered her his best *we're-a-team-here* smile.

'Hey…You're my number one *looker* out there on the counter!' he said. 'I think you just got to get into role a little more, eh?'

'Get into role?'

'Yeah, you know, a little flirty-flirty, shake your tush a bit. The customers just love that kind of thing. Makes ordering lunch a bit of fun for everyone.'

Jez shook her head. 'No, I'm not shaking my *tush*. Not with this stupid fluffy white thing on my ass.'

Noah pointed towards the counter outside his office. 'Take a look at Jules. She gets the biggest till bonus on the counter. Look…see? See…she's grabbing some sauce cartons…there…see the little wiggle? That's earning her money, girl. Every little wiggle is a bit more money in her pay check each week. That could be you, the top earner here at StarBreaks. You're my best-looking girl. You just need to grow a sense of fun.'

Jez's jaw dropped open. 'Grow a sense of fun?'

'That's right.'

'It's….demeaning.'

Noah roared with laughter. 'Demeaning?' He slapped his ample belly mirthfully then swung a thick arm around her shoulders. 'What? Did you go eat a Bill of Workers Rights for lunch? Girl, it's a bit late to be worrying about that now. You're already wearing my uniform. You're already *demeaned*. All you need to do is give a little more. That's all I'm asking. Turn it around, and make some money from it.'

Jez stared silently at him, wondering whether to lamp him one and storm out of his office with her pride intact and her head held high. Or, on the other hand, eat a little bit of pie. She knew it had to be the latter...the money at StarBreaks was too good.

Noah grew impatient with the silence. 'So, you gonna wiggle that bunny for extra money?'

Jez clenched her fists, 'hmmm, well see, the bunny tail...that's the bit I don't like, Mr Noah. I look stupid with that thing on my-'

Noah waved his hand at her irritably. He decided it was about time to wrap up this little tete-a-tete. 'Okay Jez, I'm all done being Mr NiceGuy. You either do it my way or you take the sky-way. Understand? There's only room for one loudmouth around here, and that's me.'

Jez decided to make her bid. 'How about I go and work on the deliveries?'

Noah looked bemused. 'You want to be a ped-jockey?'

'Yeah.'

Noah studied her intently. It would be a damned shame to lose a real looker like her from the counter, but then he had seen her being a little too snappy with the customers once or twice, showing them some attitude. And that wasn't being too helpful. The other girls might just pick up on that, and before he knew it they'd all be hurling their bunny tails at him.

On the other hand, that attitude of hers might better serve her down in deliveries. You needed to be a little sassy to push your way through this crowded city on a tight deadline. This girl Jez seemed like she could more than hold her own on that front. Despite being a bit of a stunner, Noah was beginning to suspect she had wa-a-ay too much attitude to be serving behind the counter. Out there delivering StarFagurters, and giving everyone else on the street some grief, she'd be a natural.

'Hey, if you're happier doing that, Jezabel, then fine.'

'That's not my name. No one calls me that,' she replied. 'It's Jez.'

CHAPTER 11

Deacon looked up from his notes sprawled across the mahogany desk and stared out at Pacifica. He rubbed his eyes, then the bridge of his nose tiredly. He knew when he'd started that this was going to turn out to be the proverbial needle in the haystack. He was looking for one candidate amongst the tens of millions of paternal applications that had passed through the laboratories during Mason's tenure as head of the Department of Genetic Analysis. He had hoped the late doctor might have been foolish enough to log somewhere in his private, locked, data directory the details of that child; a reference number, a name....something. But, having combed through the entire contents of his voluminous personal directory, it was clear that Mason hadn't.

The directory itself was full of writings and commentaries that would certainly have ended his career without question if they had been discovered whilst he was alive. He had found essays condemning virtually everything about the Administration, and, more specifically, about the dictatorial way in which paternity requests were approved, or denied. He had discovered enough material to finish the man.

If he turned up now, washed ashore on one of Pacifica's man-made atolls, he'd almost certainly wish he hadn't.

Most importantly, there was the outline of his plan….The Plan. As Deacon read through the notes, it became quickly apparent that he was glimpsing a quite brilliant mind that had gone utterly insane. What Mason had been planning for some time, would bring an end to everything. But, there was nothing in there that Deacon could see would help him find the single Paternity Request that had been dangerously altered.

The *candidate child.*

Knowing of Mason's distrust for all things modern, particularly digital records, Deacon suspected those crucial details he desperately sought might have been kept close to the old man, on his person, perhaps in an old leather-bound notebook, and now vaporised along with Mason and the other unfortunate passengers and crew aboard the shuttle.

Deacon sighed with frustration.

Since there was no knowing exactly when Mason had released his *creation* into the universe, there was also no knowing how much time they had; whether they had days, weeks, months or years to figure this thing out. The only way he could track down this child would be to look on the laboratory's main database and view all of the Paternity Requests that Mason had personally checked-out and become involved with.

He'd done that. There were seven thousand eight hundred and seventy-two applications that he had personally overseen over the last two decades.

He decided to apply some logical analysis to whittle the number down. Mason would have been very careful to select the right candidate. Deacon decided to try and get inside the Doctor's head…

He decided to start with basics. There were approximately thirteen hundred worlds, many of them could probably be ruled out as inappropriate. It was unknown to most of the greater population, but there were at least two dozen worlds right now that were in the middle of their own civil wars; these could be dismissed. There were another hundred currently policed by the Administration's soldiers where people, soldiers and civilians, were dying in their thousands from acts of terrorism and sabotage and short outbursts of insurrection that flared up from time to time. All of those strife-ridden worlds could probably be dismissed.

Of the thirteen hundred worlds there were approximately two hundred that were in the very early and dangerously unpredictable stages of environmental restructuring; *terraforming* as some people liked to refer to it. Those worlds were again too dangerous, too volatile. But on the other hand he knew Mason would surely want to pick a young world, one recently colonised, where the infrastructure of government was still yet to be fully established; a place where the comings and goings of people were not particularly well monitored. He would also want to pick a world where the process of environmental restructuring was almost complete and no major natural disasters - like those that had occurred on Celestion - might happen. Deacon guessed a stable frontier world was what Mason would have looked for. But one with enough people on it to ensure his child could migrate anonymously, slip through the nets of various government censors.

A frontier world with several large cities, a place in which a person could easily vanish for as long as they would want, that's what he would have looked for.

But that was still a very generic profile. He knew there must be several hundred that would fit that loose description. He needed to whittle that down still further.

What else? What else?

Some of those worlds could be taken out of that figure for being too remote, too far from interplanetary routes. Mason must have wanted his child to travel, to perhaps even reach the heart of Human Space, the home world of the Administration, Liberty. Other worlds could be ruled-out because of factors such as the star type and gravity which would require the candidate to be too visibly different from the *norm*. He suspected Mason wouldn't want his creation to stand out in any particular way. It would need to look utterly anonymous, unremarkable, gene-neutral…to pass through any city on any planet and not attract a second glance. A prominent or unusual skin colour, a distinctive physique, might make it noticeable, memorable in some way. The child would have to look utterly average.

What else would Mason have designed into the child?

He would surely have genetically programmed the candidate to have a desperate yearning to travel? Yes. To feel an overwhelming compulsion to be on the move, to never be content with standing still. Perhaps he would have given the child an overpowering suspicion of destiny, of fatalism….something to drive it ever onwards, to feed its nomadic urge. If he were Mason, he would have made the candidate a natural loner, socially uncomfortable, shy….so that it never made strong attachments or friendships that might anchor it to one location. Deacon would have engineered an anonymous, quiet, drifter…a ghost of a child, never noticed as it travelled the universe silently going about its mission. Never happy with where he or she was.

Deacon almost felt pity for this creature, wherever it was.

He stirred from his thoughts and decided to find where Leonard was. The young man had had several hours to study the ocean of data and try to extrapolate some useful intelligence.

He smiled proudly.

The young man was incredibly intelligent, almost a *savant* in the way he could analyze data for patterns, to distil information from chaos. The young man, still a boy really, was edgy and nervous with a mild compulsion for repetitive actions; typical indicators of a mild form of autism. Deacon had worked hard to earn the boy's trust, mentoring him patiently over several years. Leonard had proven to have an incredibly useful mind which Deacon had exploited shamelessly in his efforts to climb the ranks of Administration bureaucracy back home.

He relied on Leonard Colby, and the young man in return idolized him in an almost pathetically transparent way, as a young boy might look up to a father figure. Leonard dressed to look like Deacon, wearing clothes that aped his expensive Edwardian suits. Even attempting to grow a meagre tuft of a beard and moustache that looked like pencil lines drawn on a child's face.

Deacon was touched by the boy's imitation, and that was why it had been with some reluctance that he'd decided to bring the boy along with him.

When Mason's baby was finally located and terminated, Deacon had been given very specific instructions to ensure that all of the loose ends were tidied up. Regrettably, young Leonard would end up being one of those loose ends.

'Well Leonard? What have you got?'

'Six worlds, sir. I think it's got to be on one of these, hmmm,' the young man said holding out the shortlist for Deacon to study, his pale freckled face, looking up uncertainly at him for approval.

'Good lad. Yes…yes,' he replied stroking his chin and scanning the list. 'They all look suitable. All established frontier worlds, normal class 3 white stars, on scale 1-1 gravity.'

'They're all towards the edge of Human Space, but not right out on a limb either,' added Leonard. 'Populations vary between two and eight million people. None of these worlds have properly established central authorities; they are chaotic, badly run. Hmmm.'

'Perfect.'

Deacon reached out and patted him gently. 'Well done Leonard, I'm glad you decided to come along.'

The young man's pale face split with a proud smile.

'We need to go to work on these six worlds. We need to pull up the lab's database on Paternity Requests from these places and find out which of them Mason checked-out and had some personal involvement in, understand?'

'Of course, sir.'

Deacon looked the young man in the eye. 'And listen, Leonard?'

'Yes, sir?'

'Let's say you can call me Deacon from now on. All right? Only when we're on our own though, you understand?'

Leonard nodded, his cheeks blotched crimson. 'Yes, sir. Yes…Deacon.'

He nodded at the young man. 'Good, now let's get those details up and see how many applications we're going to have to sift through.'

Leonard nodded.

Deacon watched his young apprentice working with the display. Once this was all done and dusted, the last thing he would have to do was take this young man's life himself. Not something he was looking forward to.

'Good work, Leonard,' he said once more, patting the boy's narrow freckled neck. 'Good boy.'

CHAPTER 12

'Hi Dad, it's me.'

'Ellie? Oh, for God's sake! Ellie?'

'Yes Dad.'

'It's been nearly a month, we were getting worried!'

'I'm sorry, I'm sorry. It's just…it's these damn call-units are so expensive.'

Jacob Quin smiled sadly at her. 'I know love, I'm sorry. I…we just worry.'

'Well… look Dad, things are still okay. We're both working in a burger bar now, the money's much better than the old job. I'm serving on the counter, Jez does deliveries.'

'Jez? Is that your friend you told me about last time?'

'Yes….*Jez*. We're cube-chiks.'

'Cube-?'

'We share a cube.'

'Ah…okay. She nice?'

'She's great, Dad. Like a big sister. She's looking after me really well.'

'I'm glad,' replied Jacob. 'I'm so glad you have someone there with you.'

'Yeah, we're doing okay. Any news from Sean yet?'

'Yes. Yes, we did hear from his Dad, he got a vidmail. He's on the army planet and training hard. He asked after you. So we told his Dad to tell him that you were in New Haven and having a high old time there.'

High old time? Ellie smiled. She was doing *okay*.

'You want to speak to your Mum? She's right here.'

Maria Quin pushed Jacob out of the way. 'Ellie? How are you girl?'

'I'm good Mum, really good.'

'We're missing you Ellie. Please come home,' she said. Ellie could hear a tremble in her voice.

'I can't Mum, not for a bit. It costs too much by shuttle. But I'm saving, so maybe soon, huh?'

'I hope so. We all miss you. It feels like you're on another planet.'

I might as well be. 'How's Ted, Shona?'

'They're great. I'll shout them.'

'No! Mum, no. I gotta hang up any second, I can't wait for them. Look, give them both a kiss from me. And tell Ted I bought a Podkin.'

'A what?'

'He'll know, there's a cartoon series with them on.'

'Oh, okay.'

'I really miss you too, and I promise I'll save as much as I can and hopefully I can come out and see you soon,' said Ellie, realising that was a rash promise.

'Please do my love,' said Maria.

'Okay, I have to go Mum…this is costing.'

'Yes dear, I understand.'

'Love you.'

'We love you too.'

Ellie watched the grainy vid-image of her parents waving frantically flicker and fade as she disconnected the call. It suddenly sounded very quiet inside the cube. Jez was on her shift and the toob was turned off for once. The only noises she could hear were the rumble of airborne traffic outside, the faint warble of a marshal's siren bouncing off the tenement towers and the distant clacking of someone's heels in the passageway beyond their cube door.

Not for the first time, she looked at the scuffed plastic walls of their little cube and felt like a podkin herself.

*

Jez gunned the throttle on her d-ped as she sped down the pedestrian walkway en route to her second delivery of four. This one still had just under five minutes on the delivery-promise timer. She had to deliver it to a habi-cube on the fifth floor of New Hampshire Tower.

Jez weaved around several clusters of pedestrians who made little or no effort to move aside for her.

'Yeah, thanks a freg,' she shouted out as she whizzed past, flipping a finger at them.

New Hampshire Tower lay dead ahead, a bronze coloured cone that shimmered in the late afternoon haze. She noticed there were several ramps up to a raised pedestrian plaza, approximately twelve stories up.

Take the ramp up, and an elevator down to the fifth...quickest way.

She leant to her left, swung off the crowded ground-level street and took the ramp upwards. The d-ped whined with a higher pitch at the upward incline. Jez cursed the StarBreaks mechanic for equipping her d-ped with a duff thruster unit.

As she climbed upwards along the ramp, by-passing a grossly overweight couple that were wheezing and puffing from the exertion, she cast a glance outwards across the urban carpet sliding away below her. She looked for her next delivery location; Law

Marshall Precinct 76. Jez quickly spotted the rotating blue holographic sign, a shield, but couldn't see the squat precinct building itself. She checked the display on the saddle between her legs; the third order still had twelve minutes on it.

More than enough time.

As she drew up towards the plaza above her, she cast a glance to the left at the bronze semi-reflective portholes whipping past her. She loved snatching a glimpse into other people's cubes. As each porthole passed, she caught a momentary snapshot of other private lives; a young buck standing naked in his bedroom, staring out. The next window…a family with young children, all of them staring listlessly at their toob; a man and woman fingers raised at each other, clearly in the middle of a row; another couple staring at the toob, and another, and another.

She turned to look where she was going, just as the d-ped came to the end of the rising ramp and rolled onto the plaza. It was just like any other mid-level pedestrian platform; a few shops, a fast food joint, milling people and more importantly, entrances to the tenement towers that surrounded it. She spotted the New

Hampshire entrance and weaved across the plaza towards it.

As she drove into the entrance she spotted a sign on the wall forbidding the use of d-peds and other micro-vehicles inside.

'Yeah, right,' she muttered as she rolled inside towards a row of lifts within the foyer. She hit one of the lift's buttons and then checked the saddle display once more.

Three minutes and fifty-five seconds.

Loads of time.

She looked up when she heard the ping, only to see a Law Marshal coming out.

'Hey! Take that outside, before I impound it,' he said gruffly.

Jez cursed under her breath. The chances of running into a marshal in the street were pretty damned low, let alone one actually bothering to visit a tenement tower. She spun the bike round and prepared to take it out.

'Walk it out!' the marshal called after her.

Jez slid off the saddle and wheeled it outside, muttering through gritted teeth as she did so. She leaned the d-ped against the wall and then opened the warm-box to pull out the order.

'Hey, marshal guy!' she called out as the Law Marshal emerged from the entrance beside her. 'Could you watch this for a minute?'

He turned towards her and walked over. 'A minute you say?'

'That's it. I'll be right up.'

'Sure yeah, alright then,' he said nodding.

Jez slapped his arm, 'thanks.'

'Hey chik, want me to wax it for you too?'

Jez stopped, realising there was a hint of irony in his voice. 'You're not actually going to watch it, are you?'

'What do you think?' he said shaking his head and laughing as he turned to walk away.

'Well can you just hang around the plaza for a minute? Go get a doughnut or something,' she called out after him.

The marshal looked sternly back at her over his shoulder for a moment before proceeding on his way.

With one last, hasty look around, Jez took the StarBreaks order inside, ran across the foyer to the lifts and dived into the first one that arrived. She jabbed at the fifth floor button and cursed with frustration as it slowly rumbled downwards. The doors eventually slid open and she ran out into a passageway lined with the numbered oval doors of habi-cubes.

Number 157 was towards the other end. Of course it was. She set off at a sprint, counting down the last minute in her head as she did so. She reached the habi-cube as she hit the last twenty seconds and pressed her palm against the door-chime.

As she counted down the last ten she heard some movement from inside and finally the door hissed open.

'Your StarBreaks order, ma'am,' said Jez breathlessly.

The woman standing in the doorway looked at the order with an expression of disdain. 'You're late. I'm not paying for that.'

'No. Actually, I'm not. I'm exactly on time. To within five seconds in fact,' replied Jez, her face stiffening with irritation.

'It's late I tell you. I timed this order on my own clock. And it says you're late.'

Yeah, like hell you did.

'Well according to my clock it's on time ma'am, and therefore a refund doesn't apply.'

The woman reached out and grabbed the order. 'Fregg it, I'll have it anyway. But I won't be using StarBreaks anymore.'

Jez tried to contain her disappointment. 'No?'

'No,' she replied. 'You took far too long.'

She sighed. 'Just to be clear…you really won't call StarBreaks again?'

'No! Never!'

Jez smiled. *Good*. 'In that case, I hope you choke on it you miserable, ugly, fat mother-freggin' bitch.'

The woman's eyes widened.

'That's right. Enjoy eating that crap. You really wouldn't want to know what goes into it, but I'll tell you this for nothing…I spat in it, so did the food-order chef, and several of the other girls in the back kitchen. Enjoy.'

Jez emerged from New Hampshire running as fast as she could. By her calculation she was going to have to make up some time for the next delivery to the Law Marshal's precinct building.

Relieved to see it still resting against the wall, she jumped astride the d-ped and pushed the joystick down.

Nothing happened.

She tried again, but the thruster didn't even offer its trademark throaty cough. She turned round in her saddle to give the damned thing a well-deserved slap, only to find the propulsion unit was gone. 'Ahh, what the fuggin-shizt! I don't believe it!

Somebody had lifted it.

She looked around for the marshal she'd spoken to earlier. Nowhere to be seen of course. She checked her saddle display again. She still had five minutes left on the next order and twelve on the final one.

If she missed on both of those Noah would chew her out big time. Thrusters were cheap enough, but losing a big order to the local Law Marshal precinct - and those boys in there really enjoyed their fast food - would mean losing a lot of repeat business.

She had no choice.

'I ...I...I...UGHH!!!!' Jez growled with frustration, smacking her fist against the wall several times, climbed off, went round the back and detached the warm-box. Then she unclipped the saddle display. Carrying the box under one arm and holding the display in her other hand, she jogged across the plaza towards the ramp she had come up only minutes earlier, and began to make her way down to street level.

She reached the street with only four minutes left on the next order and carried on jogging as best she could between the milling pedestrians, anxiously glancing at the display every few seconds.

The Law Marshal building was only two or three hundred yards down the street on the right. As she weaved in and out of the crowd, she caught the occasional glance of the rotating blue holographic display between the flitting aircars and rumbling skyhounds descending down to street level to drop off and pick up.

She looked down once more at the display…*three minutes.*

And then all of a sudden, she was flat on her face, the warm-box skittering across the plastimac pavement, kicked around accidentally several times by the passing forest of legs.

'Oh for f-….what now?!' Jez howled with frustration.

She looked around to see what she had tripped over. It was a construction jimp. It cowered guiltily on the ground surrounded by a ring of marking tape clearly warning passersby of 'maintenance work in progress'. It watched her warily, its two all-black eyes nervously darting one way then the other in a face with no nose and a slit for a mouth. Above its eyes, on the forehead, Jez could see the manufacturer's logo 'GenIndo' in a dark blue pigment that stood out crisply from the jimp's pale corn-yellow skin tone.

Jez angrily made a move towards the creature, raising one leg to deliver a swift, hard kick. As she did so, it curled its four arms around its head and curled into a vaguely foetal position. Jez hesitated. She knew Ellie felt sorry for these pathetic automatons. She hated the way people in the city casually lashed out at them for little or no reason, often just for laughs. Ellie said she thought that was because people like to kick at something they considered to be lower down the pecking order than their selves; jimps fulfilled that role nicely. Jez lowered her foot to the floor. Maybe Crazy-Ellie was right. Maybe these poor little freaks had a tough enough time as it was, without her adding to it.

Jez nodded at the creature, and muttered a chastened 'sorry' before dusting herself off and retrieving the warm-box that had been kicked to the side of the street. She cast one more glance back at the creature. It had resumed its task of digging an access hole in the ground to some junction box or other. Jez was bemused by Ellie's attitude towards jimps. Being a farm-chik she was probably unused to being around them, not really aware that they were little more than genetically engineered construction tools. Organic robots.

She shook her head. Ellie was a funny girl sometimes.

Two minutes left on the order. If she picked up the pace and this time kept an eye on the damned street ahead, she calculated she might just about make it in time.

She barged her way through a tight knot of people waiting patiently to squeeze through a narrow bottleneck in the street, receiving a salvo of curses in return. Finally pushing herself out through the other side and disentangling herself from them, she could see the precinct building directly ahead of her. It was a low box-shaped, dirty, plasteel structure squatting in the shadows of a tower either side and a pedestrian plaza some fifty feet above it. Hidden from the filtered afternoon sun in this permanent semi-darkness, it looked like a forgotten box-shaped toadstool living at the base of some giant trees.

She redoubled her flagging pace, her breath rasping and coarse from the exertion of her four and a half minute sprint down from the New Hampshire tower. Last time she had been this out of breath the man trapped beneath her had begged her to let him go.

Her feet pounded the pavement with the determined rhythmic *clack* of her platform boots.

She threw one more, hasty glance at the display…it was counting down the last minute.

Come on, you lazy thigh-slapper!

She picked up the speed once more, closing the final hundred yards with an athletic sprint that drew a passing glance of curiosity from the shuffling pedestrians she swept by.

She took the three steps leading up to the building's entrance at a leap and burst inside through plastic-flap draft excluders that swung in noisily, slapping and scraping across the grimy vinyl floor as Jez collapsed across several orange bucket-seats opposite the entrance.

The marshal standing behind the glass security-screen above the counter recoiled in shock at her explosive entrance.

'What the…?' his voice crackled over the speakers on Jez's side of the screen.

Jez bent over double, fighting for breath for a moment before pulling the battered and dented warm-box out from under her arm. She opened it wordlessly and presented it towards the officer behind the screen.

He looked at the churned-up mess inside, lit by the flickering blue tube light above the counter. He wrinkled his nose. 'And this is?'

Jez took another moment to catch her breath before offering up a reply. 'Four Double-slab StarGurters, a Star-Proti-beef Rib salad, five orders of StarCarboCurls, and three white coffees.'

The marshal studied the contents in silence, then finally shook his head. 'Uhh...not any more it isn't.'

OMNIPEDIA:
[Human Universe digital encyclopedia]

Article: Ellie Quin > Myths from New Haven

The story of Ellie Quin, being so poorly documented, is predictably confused by many myths and fictions that have grown and evolved over the centuries. They serve to drown out what we *really* know about her with tales we would perhaps like to believe.

So let's have a look at some of the more established myths.

One of the earliest to come out of New Haven not many years after Ellie's death was that of the *alien fortune teller*. For many people, this myth expanded and became folklore. The myth changed over generations, mutating into various different versions, in some cases becoming the cornerstone of some minor cult-like faiths. One has to dig deep though to find the original tale.

The original tale goes something like this;- that during the period of time Ellie

Quin stayed in this long gone city, she visited a fortune teller, an alien. It was a member of the now extinct species referred to back then as a *Boojam*. The myth relates how the alien foretold her future in precise detail. That looking only into her eyes, it could foresee the enormity of her destiny, what awaited her and what awaited all of mankind, and then proceeded to explain this to her. So it is said, from that moment on, she was a woman with a mission, with an understanding of what she had to do, and most importantly, a woman with certain knowledge that she would one day have to give her life to save humanity.

It is tempting to believe that the fascinating story of Ellie Quin's life was somehow authored by her foreknowledge of the destiny that awaited her; that every decision she made in her tragically short life was intentional, driven by what she knew lay ahead. Driven by what she knew she had to do.

Another popular myth that emerged from the city in the years after The Event was the *Crusade Myth*. The myth tells how she led a crusade through those ancient city streets, a crusade that united the poor, the disenfranchised, the ill and the infirm against the greedy corporations and the money-makers who ensured that the people of Harpers Reach were anchored to servitude by poverty and debt.

A third story tells of how, in the short period of time that she lived in the city, Ellie Quin amassed a fortune by setting up and running a business empire that spanned the planet. That she ruled the world for a few short years, setting to right all the evil that she found in the two cities. The tale goes on to tell how she grew weary of her fabulous wealth and power and left Harpers Reach for the wilderness and anonymity of space to discover her greater destiny.

There is no real evidence of *any* of these myths having any basis in truth. If one were pushed to favor a particular story as being vaguely plausible, one might gravitate towards the crusade myth. The 'fortune-teller', 'divine inspiration' and the 'rags to riches to rags' concepts are oft-used fables that date back as far as the Old Earth Christian bible, and beyond, and have been more than likely appropriated and adjusted to feature Ellie Quin in the starring role.

In all honesty, all of those myths are just that….just stories. We know nothing certain about her time in New Haven, other than, at some point, she finally made it out of the city and eventually off-world.

User Comment > Digi-EeZee

She never existed people! Don't you see? She's a made-up thing; like Wintersaurus, The Egg Fairy, Sean the Mystic Snail. SHE NEVER EXISTED!

User Comment > Herod889

I believe in her. I believe in her. I believe in her. I believe in her. I believe in her. I believe in her. I believe in her. I believe in her. I beli **[message characters deleted]**

User Comment > n00b-boob

Zealots. *sigh*

CHAPTER 13.

'It's a revolutionary new drink. This is going to change how we, as a species, view liquid consumption!' the young woman announced, holding the moment for as long as possible so that her assembled audience could truly understand the magnitude of her statement.

Ellie shuffled uncomfortably as the speaker, a smartly presented business woman who had energetically introduced herself as *Juliette*, momentarily locked eyes on her, before moving on to stare intently at someone else behind her.

This had been Jez's idea, of course. She had spotted the holographic advert drifting across the street like a lost balloon whilst out and looking for work. Being fired so publicly from StarBreaks a few days earlier seemed to have put a small dent in the self assurance she wore like a force field around herself, and Jez was eagerly looking for a quick opportunity to bounce back spectacularly and prove to the world, perhaps more so to Ellie, that she was a trooper; a survivor who really didn't need a cruddy job in a burger bar. Jez said she was tired of working for other people anyway and had announced that she thought it was about time that she, and Ellie, worked for themselves.

So it was no surprise that she had been immediately seduced by the promise on the floating billboard of fabulous wealth within only a few weeks. It made no mention of exactly how such an unlikely thing would come to pass, just that it almost certainly would….and of course, offered a number to call for those who were interested.

'So…you want to know, don't you? You want to know what it is?' asked Juliette rhetorically, her voice dropping to the hushed whisper of a conspirator. With a flourish of a well-manicured hand, she hit a button on the lectern beside her. All of a sudden the walls of the small conference cube were alive with the projected images of the most beautiful young people Ellie had ever seen. They were laughing, smiling, frolicking in the tumbling surf of some tropical world, playing games, passing a ball to each other gaily, rolling seductively in the purest white sand. And all of these beautiful people, it seemed, had an insatiable taste for the same brand of bottled drink - a tall, thin

143

bottle with a blue and orange logo spiralling around it. She watched as flashing images of these adorable people enjoying this drink, slurping from the bottles and smiling, exposing impossibly white teeth, flickered across the walls.

'I give you *Spectora*!' cried Juliette spreading her arms with an infectious, evangelistic outpouring of excitement and wonder. 'Spectora, ladies and gentlemen…it's not just a sodapop, it's not just a way of life. It's the future.'

Ellie glanced at Jez. She was grinning like a simpleton. But then, this woman, Juliette, had had Jez hooked from 'Good Morning' – she'd been all ready and set to buy into this even before the sales pitch had begun.

'Now, I'm sure you're wondering what makes Spectora different to any other bottled drink out there aren't you?' She turned away from the flickering images on the walls to face them. 'Any of you care to take a guess?' she asked, her eyes scanning the audience.

There was a prolonged silence.

'Come on, don't be shy, anyone?'

Ellie hunched down ever so slightly in her seat, hoping the broad, slope-shouldered man in front of her would provide enough of a shield to hide her from this woman's piercing eyes. Juliette slowly tracked left-to-right along the front three rows, relentlessly towards Ellie.

Agghh...don't pick me, don't pick me, don't pick...

'How about you young man? You're not hiding from me now, are you?' she said leaning to one side and looking around the man in front of Ellie. 'Come on then, Mr Hide-n-Seek.'

'Uh, I'm...err...I'm not a man.'

Juliette frowned, took a step forward. 'Oh, yes. You're not, are you? Sorry.' She shrugged like it was forgotten already. 'So what do you think it is about Spectora that makes it so special?'

Ellie's pale face instantly coloured. Rose-tinted blotches blossomed across her cheeks. 'Uh...I...I really....I...I'm not sure,' she stammered awkwardly, and then thought up an answer just to get her off the hook. She knew it was pretty lame as she said it. 'Because it's really fizzy?'

Jez shook her head with pity and *tutted* out loud at Ellie's answer. She thrust her hand into the air and bobbed up and down on her seat, eager to catch the woman's attention.

'Yes?'

'Is it the taste, Juliette? It IS isn't it?' Jez announced loudly. 'It's the taste.'

Juliette nodded and her lips spread with a smile. 'You are a very perceptive young woman! That's right, it IS all in the taste. Let's have a round of applause for our smart young sales candidate here,' she said pointing at Jez.

The other members of the audience, twenty or thirty people, clapped dutifully as Jez stood up and took a theatrical bow before sitting down again as the muted applause quickly died out. Ellie hunched stiffly in her chair, annoyed with herself for sounding like an utter dudhead and for being so damned self-conscious and shy.

'Now, I want you to look at all these beautiful young people in the infomercial. They're all drinking our wonderful Spectora, but have you noticed anything else?'

This time mercifully Juliette didn't bother looking for someone else to skewer publicly. 'There's only *one* bottle. One flavour. Spectora only comes in one, *wonderful* flavour. Who would like to try it?'

Jez's arm shot up again. 'I'll give it a go!'

Ellie sighed. Jez was as unbearably excitable as usual. Her obsessive desire to be

146

the centre of attention could be somewhat wearing, especially when she was on a roll. She was even worse after a few Spartans.

Juliette pulled a bottle out from behind her lectern and came towards them. She pressed down on the top of the plastic bottle and popped the seal with an audible hiss, before handing it to Jez.

'Tell me what you think,' she said nodding knowingly to the rest of the audience with an expectant just-you-wait-for-it grin spreading across her lips

Jez stood up again so that everyone could see her, reached out for the bottle and took a hearty swig, turning to mug at everyone else as she did so.

Ellie rolled her eyes. *Oh please.*

A moment passed as Jez theatrically swilled the liquid around in her mouth and swallowed.

'Well?' asked Juliette.

Jez nodded. 'It's nice. Sort of tastes a bit like…chocolate…no...'

Juliette winked at the audience as Jez's eyebrows knotted in concentration.

'No, it's more like, wow! It just changed to taste like, like….like a fruity, no, hang on, there it goes again! It's...it's changing. It's-'

Juliette waved for her to sit down again, which Jez did reluctantly.

'Ladies and gentleman, Spectora uses a revolutionary new technique that our men in lab coats call 'evolutionary bacterial warfare'. It's really very, very clever, and I'm going to explain to you,' she said raising two fingers on each hand to do air quotes, 'the *science* bit.'

CHAPTER 14

Jez was in her element. Of course she was. Street-selling was definitely *her* thing, Ellie noted with a resigned shrug. Selling and flirting…that's what she was born to do.

'You see, it contains two very different strains of micro-organisms that react violently against each other,' said Jez as she handed the free sample bottle to the old man she had cornered. 'Go on, take a sip…just for me,' she added with a wink and pursing her full lips ever so slightly.

The non-so subtle suggestive pout worked. The man took the bottle from her, cracked the seal and took a hesitant sip.

'You'll feel the liquid hit your tongue and immediately there's a taste isn't there?'

The man nodded. 'Yeah, what's that?...vanilla?'

'But then it changes, from second to second, becoming another, entirely different flavour in an instant.'

'Yeah, you're right,' he said, a look of surprise on his face.

'I'll tell you what's happening,' continued Jez, effortlessly regurgitating the Spectora *sales shtick* they had been handed by Juliette yesterday. 'Right now there are two colonies of micro-organisms fighting a desperate war of survival across your tongue. Your mouth is a battlefield, your taste buds…command and control points and both those bacterial armies are fighting ferociously for control of them. As the casualties fluctuate throughout this microcosmic war so the chemical balance of the drink changes and thus so does the flavour.'

'Crud!' said the man, swilling the liquid around,' that's …I just got a taste of munge-mellow in there for a second!'

Jez smiled. 'It really is an amazing drink isn't it?'

The man nodded, silently enjoying the continuing montage of sugary flavours in his mouth.

'This is the drink of the future. It's new, it's fun, it's exciting and it's going to kick all the other bottled drinks out of the market. So, why not join me and the Spectora family? You could become your own boss, a licensed vendor and make a fortune, like I'm doing right now, selling this wonderful new drink!'

Jez moved in closer to him, her voice lowered ever so slightly. 'In a matter of weeks, you could be earning thousands of creds a day. And in turn, not only will you earn money selling Spectors yourself, but also you could earn five percent from the sales of any new vendors you bring into the family.'

'Really?'

'Oh yeah. If you manage to recruit four or five people to sell Spectora, and they in turn each do the same, pretty soon you won't even need to bother selling it yourself anymore! They'll be making your money for you. How's that for a great deal?!'

The man nodded. 'Yeah, yeah, I see what you mean.'

'Good! I mean, it makes sense doesn't it? Why not take this opportunity now? Be one of the first to become an *Spectora Ambassador*?'

Ellie watched the man's eyes lighting up. Jez had got her hooks into the poor guy. He wasn't going to walk away now, he was on the line and she was reeling him in. Another guaranteed sale for Jez.

'Okay...so uh, how do I join, this...uh, *family*?'

Jez presented him with a card. 'This is my agency number. You call the number on this card, quote the agency number, and for a small fee that covers the training day, you can become one of my licensed vendors. Easy as easy-peas.'

The man took the card, smiling. 'Thank you...thanks!' he said grasping Jez's hand. 'Really? You think I'll be making thousands of creds?'

'Sure!' Jez grinned and shook his hand. 'Let's do business together soon, eh?' she added with another suggestive wink. 'The sooner the better. Remember, you want to be one of the first, don't you?'

'Yeah, I...s'pose I guess I do.'

'Well you get home right now and call that number. Do it as fast as you can. I want *you* to be one of the first on my team, okay?'

The man nodded obediently and turned on his heels. Jez watched him walking briskly away swigging some more of the drink from the free sampler bottle and intently studying the business card she had given him. Then she turned towards Ellie standing sullenly beside her.

'How do you do it?' asked Ellie. 'I can't seem to get *anyone* to stop and have a go, let alone get them to sign up with me.'

Jez shrugged. 'You just got to keep trying, Ellie. It's all about getting your teeth into them and then hanging on. Wait…these ones look good, here we go.'

Ellie studied her friend as she moved out into the stream of walking traffic again and blocked the way of some more hapless pedestrians.

This is what she does best.

She watched Jez, dressed in her Spectora sales uniform; a tight-fitting orange, neoprene-rubber mini-dress with the logo winding diagonally down the front, and a blue bell-boy's cap tilted at a jaunty angle on top of her head. Ellie grimaced. Basically, not to put too fine a point on it - they were dressed up to look like giant bottles of the stupid drink.

How come she doesn't feel like a complete gaga dressed like this?

Ellie shook her head in wonder and admiration. She watched enviously as Jez coerced both men into giving it a try. A second ago they'd looked as if nothing would stop them going where they needed to be. And then they had run headlong into Jez, whose sales pitch appeared to be a seamless blend of overbearing pushiness and shameless flirtation.

Ellie caught a reflection of herself in the shop window across the busy street.

Look at me. She saw a plain, skinny girl with a miserable face that looked like a slapped arse…dressed up to look like a plastic bottle of pop.

What the hell am I doing?

They had been here all morning, since the first early risers had started spilling out onto the lowest ground levels, and Ellie had failed to convince a single person to give the damned drink a try. Jez on the other hand had managed to stop pretty much every person she had accosted, and then of those, easily half of them had walked away clutching her card like found money.

The woman at the seminar yesterday, Juliette, had confidently assured them both that once they got out into the street in their sales costumes and started with the sales patter, Spectora would sell itself.

Yeah…a real breeze for Jez maybe. Not for her though.

She sighed miserably. The vending franchise that both of them had bought, which included the costumes, the business cards, a start-up stock of the drink and some odds and ends of promotional material, had cost them two hundred and fifty creds each.

154

That had pretty much wiped her out. Jez had talked her into spending what little money she had managed to scrimp and save over the last few months, to buy a franchise, promising they'd make that money back within days.

Crud. Jez was utterly froob-head over this. By the end of yesterday's seminar she was well and truly sucked in, ready to throw the last of their money at becoming Spectora Ambassadors. Well, it looked like it was working out for *her* alright, but for Ellie this was looking like a complete disaster. She was reminded of some nursery tale her mother had read her long ago about a boy foolishly selling his cow for some magic beans.

Jez returned across the street to Ellie. 'Come on sales-chik, you've got to look like you're having *fun*. Like you're all happy-clappy. No-one's going to stop for you with a face like that!' said Jez shaking her head disapprovingly.

Ellie looked at her wearily. 'It's as easy as that? I just smile a lot? Come on Jez, it's more than that. *You* can do it, you can get people to buy things, because....'

'Because what?'

'Because…because you look good. And you damn well know that! The men sign up because you do that kissy-kissy thing with your lips, and the women because….'

Jez shrugged, 'because?'

Ellie struggled to find the words. 'Because…I don't know, maybe because they want to be like you or something. I don't know. It's hard to…I guess you've either got it or you haven't. And I definitely haven't.'

Jez came over and put an arm around her. 'Ellie girl, it's not about how *sexy* you are. It's about how *confident* you are. And throwing on a smile is just about the most important bit. It tells people that you *own* the ground you're standing on.' Jez gestured to the pedestrians passing them, some curiously glancing their way. 'Look at them, Ellie. None of them smiling, none of them. That's because they're all terrified.'

'Terrified?'

'Yeah….insecure. Afraid of standing out from the herd. Maybe because they don't want to be razzed by some street-hoods, or pulled aside by some law marshal, or even worse than either of those - approached by some smiling stranger dressed like a bottle of pop and actually being *spoken* to! They're afraid to be *embarrassed*.'

Ellie could sort of understand that, actually.

'But you know what?' Jez continued evangelising.

'What?'

'Something I've worked out in my head. Deep down, they want to smile too, but they're looking for someone to do it first, to - I don't know, to give them permission.'

Ellie looked at her friend with an expression of cynicism. 'You've been watching too much Dr FixHeart on the toob.'

Jez laughed. 'Yeah that did sound a bit paffy. But seriously Ellie-girl, try it out for yourself. Just throw on a smile and see where that gets you.'

Ellie studied her reflection, aware that those passing by were watching her out of the corners of their eyes, watching the daft skinny girl with the stupid bottle-dress on.

Awkwardly, self-consciously, Ellie forced a smile onto her lips.

'There! See? Now already you look a whole lot different to all these miserable ditto-heads walking past us. I mean, look! Miserable freggers, the lot of them,' Jez muttered quietly. 'And wow, Ellie….you look about a billion times prettier! You should do the smile-thing more often, girl,' said Jez digging her in the ribs and laughing. 'Come on, wider smile…show some pearlies.'

The taut, manic smile that she had stretched across her lips felt utterly false and uncomfortable. She wondered how the hell Jez could keep it up for hours on end; one big plastic phoney smile.

But, Ellie noticed, she was right about something. One of the people passing in front of her had looked up, hesitantly met her eyes and smiled uncertainly back.

There it was again, another momentary, faltering, restrained smile from someone she had never met before in her life. Maybe Jez was right. Maybe such a pointless, insincere gesture was all it took; all that stood between her and making a fortune.

'You're doing well, girl,' said Jez still watching her. 'Now how do you feel?'

How do I feel? Like a damned ploob-head…

No – hang on, she didn't.

To Ellie's astonishment, for the first time that morning, she didn't feel like an utter freak. Grinning like this, like a mindless fool…there was something about this stupid, inane grinning thing that seemed to be cancelling-out her painful embarrassment. It was almost as if her face was telling everyone else;

I really don't care what you think I look like, I __know__ I look just peachy.

Jez gently nudged her forwards. 'Okay sales-chik, now it's all about confidence. Brassing it out. Don't wander out there and sheepishly ask whether they *might* like to try a sip. You've got to go out there and *demand* it!' said Jez. 'So, come on then.'

'Now?'

'Yes, now.'

Ellie looked once more at her reflection across the street. Yes, now she looked like another person entirely; in a way, a bit more like Jez, like someone who knows exactly who they are and where they're headed. She felt okay, not the humble, wretched creature she felt like the rest of the time.

Faking it. Faking being confident. But that's okay. That's what other 'super-confident' people do. Right?

'All right,' she said. 'I'm ready.'

She took several steps forward towards the river of people passing down the street, the smile still frozen upon her lips, and then she picked out a man walking towards her, his eyes, like everyone else's, cast down and glazed over. Ellie planted her feet in front of him and at the last moment the man stopped and looked up.

'Hi,' she said.

'Whuh?'

For a moment the sales pitch that she had spent last night rehearsing and role-playing with Jez had vanished from her mind, but then the *opener* came to her rescue.

'Would you like to be one of the first to join me, and make a thousand creds a week?' she gushed enthusiastically.

'Whuh?' he grunted again.

'Make a tho-u-u-s-a-and creds a week?' she repeated, mimicking Jez's drawled delivery.

The man shrugged, suspiciously curious.

Ellie turned uncertainly to Jez, unsure what to say next, but Jez flapped her hands frantically for her to rattle-on with the pitch. She quickly turned back to face him, fearful of losing the momentum.

'Yes! Of course you would! I'm Ellie by the way, and I'm well on the way to earning that sort of money. And I'm doing it selling this wonderful, revolutionary, new drink - SPECTORA!'

The man looked dead pan. His shoulders shrugged a 'so what'. She could see with that announcement his momentary curiosity was satisfied. *So you sell bottled pop, I get it. Big deal.*

'I want you to try just one sip, sir.....just for me. Because, that's all it's going to take to totally change your life. Just one little sip.'

'Uh no, thanks,' he said looking to step around her.

Ellie's smile faltered with frustration. *Come on Ellie, think of something girl. Don't let your first prospect go.*

'One little sip,' she pursed her lips ever so slightly, the way she had seen Jez do a million times, and winked. 'I'm sure I won't disappoint you.'

The man stopped and his eyes darted over her, lingering on her flat chest, her legs and her face, in that order - appraising her in the space of a heartbeat. It made her skin crawl.

'Okay, guess. Just for you chik,' he replied cracking the faint beginnings of a smile.

Ellie whipped out a bottle of Spectora, popped the seal and thrust it towards him. 'With this first taste, I assure you, things will never be the same,' she said, the foolish leer on her face beginning to cause her cheeks to ache. 'You and me are gonna be business partners.'

She cringed inside. His eyebrows flickered hopefully, as once more his gaze ran up her legs to her face, in one evaluating sweep and then finally to the bottle of pop in front of him. He reached out for it.

'Tell me what flavour you think it is, okay?' she said.

He nodded. 'Whatever,' and then casually chugged a mouthful from the bottle. He swilled it around his mouth for a moment before his face locked into an expression of concentration.

'That's pretty good….what is that? A sort of ice-cream flavour?'

Ellie nodded. 'Could be….what else?'

His eyes widened with surprise as inside his mouth micro-bacterial war raged and the casualties on both sides began mounting up. 'Hey, the flavour just changed, now it's sort of….what?...sort of, fruity I think.'

Oh God! I think I've got a customer!

Ellie laughed. 'Great isn't it? It just keeps changing from second to second.'

The man took a second mouthful and once more swilled it around his mouth. 'Boy…there's another flavour coming through. Its….woah…weird….sort of a savoury flavour?'

Savoury? That was odd, she thought. So far the various sensations she had heard people announcing on trying the drink had all been sweet and sugary. The one bottle from their start-up stock she had consumed last night with Jez had been a kaleidoscope of sugary, fruity, creamy flavours. No savoury ones though.

The man's nose wrinkled slightly. 'Euuch….sort of meaty….smokey, like flame-grilled proto-meat. That's, just…are you sure that's right?' The man looked at her with an expression of bemusement, that quickly evolved into nascent disgust. 'Ughh, this is turning…! It tastes like – like –' he looked up at her. 'Like shit!'

'Oh come on. It's not that bad, is it?'

'No I mean it actually tastes like faeces, you know? Really, like shit.'

Ellie's smile suddenly felt out of place as he spat the drink out onto the ground. 'You're kidding me right?' He sputtered. 'You're earning a thousand creds a week selling this bottled arse cream?'

'Um, yeah, it's…uhh…it's really popular,' she muttered.

'Achhh. I can still fregging taste it! Have you got any water so I can rinse my mouth out?'

'Errr…no, sorry,' she answered. 'So you umm, you really *don't* like it, I guess?'

'Are you kidding?' he said, and then retched. 'Uhhh, this is disgusting. Really…oh man, I think I'm going to hewdle!'

The man pushed past Ellie and lurched to the side of the street. He bent over a pile of rubbish and splattered it with a hosing of vomit.

Ellie looked at Jez, who had frozen mid-sales pitch and watched the man bent double, heaving and retching painfully. Jez looked at her, eyes widened, as if to say *what did you just do to him?*

The man finally took a moment to fight back the nausea and look up at Ellie. 'You! You crazy stupid bitch! What the fregg is that stuff?'

Ellie looked back at Jez, wondering what the exit strategy was. A spasm caused the man to shudder and he vomited again. After he had finished jettisoning another load, he turned back and took a couple of menacing steps towards her.

'I'm going to get a fregging marshal on to you girl! Somebody call a marshal!' he shouted out dizzily, dropping to one knee and clutching his guts. 'The bitch just poisoned me. Get a marshal!!'

She looked back at Jez again. This time Jez nodded and both girls turned on their heels and ran.

*

The news on the toob was not something Jez bothered with often, if at all. She preferred the shopping channels interspersed with a regular diet of sopa-drams and quizzies. But this evening Ellie had flipped the holo display to New Haven's main news channel and Jez on this occasion was more than happy to scan the news along with her.

'Nothing so far,' said Ellie. 'Maybe we're okay.'

They sat on their jel couch in the darkness, lit only by the cyan glow of the toob. For some reason this evening they'd both decided to leave the light off in the main cube and cowered in the flickering blue light of the holo-display like a pair of convicts on the run.

'Maybe he didn't manage to call a marshal then,' said Jez. 'I mean you can never find one when you want one, can you?'

'He looked pretty sick Jez. What if I…you know? Killed him?'

Jez looked at the three boxes of soft drink in the corner. 'You didn't kill him Ellie. If anything happened to him, like, well…say like he died, then it wasn't *your* fault. He might have had some really weird, really rare allergy or something.'

'Oh crud, Jez. I hope he's okay.'

'I'm sure it's just…'

The news story that had been on, a demonstration by migrants from Celestion down by the southern gate that had turned nasty after some law marshals had arrived and exercised some zero-tolerance attitude, was replaced with a white and orange product logo that silenced Jez instantly

'Today in the Service Sector a man was taken seriously ill after being sold a bottle of an unapproved soft drink known as 'Spectora'. The drink, a product of un-licensed genetic engineering, possibly by a factory on Harpers Reach, or off-world, has been noted on several other worlds in this sector. The company behind the drink, Flexegen, has no registered headquarters on

Harpers Reach, but is known to be operating here. Administration information on the company has revealed that it is believed to be a commercial money-laundering enterprise, to process and also raise funds for various terrorist groups…'

Ellie looked at Jez, 'oh crud.'

'…*The man is said to be in a serious but stable condition, but law marshals offered this warning to people today…*' The image on the display changed to show a middle-aged, middle-ranking marshal speaking. *'This drink is not approved by the Administration and, as we've seen today, contains potentially lethal and active genetically engineered ingredients. If you see a bottle of this stuff, or see someone selling it, you should contact the nearest marshal immediately. We will make every effort to find and arrest the organisers behind this illegal product, and the dealers who have been selling it on the street. Thank you.'*

Jez muted the toob. It was now showing flickering images of the teen singer Betsy Boomalackah visiting some venue over in Harvest City to promote her latest track. Jez pointed towards the boxes of drink, their Spectora uniforms, the business cards and

167

sales materials. 'Where's the nearest rubbish incinerator?'

'Up two floors.'

'Let's go.'

CHAPTER 15

Deacon studied the data files that had been compiled for him by Leonard. There were six planets the young lad had short-listed as the most likely places that Mason would have selected for the candidate. For each of these planets Leonard had noted all the paternity requests that Mason had personally checked out and had done something with to do with over the last twenty years. The list of names was long, over a thousand of them, and they were dispersed across five different worlds. And these five worlds were dotted right across Human Space.

He sat back in the leather chair and cursed. What he wouldn't give to have five minutes alone with that madman Mason, and something sharp to prod him with. When he had started rooting through the old man's things, he'd had high hopes that somewhere Mason would have slipped up and left a detail, a clue, a fragment of data that would, with a little lateral thinking, lead him directly to the candidate child.

But he hadn't.

The late doctor had been very careful to ensure nothing that could lead him to the child was digitally stored. Deacon had to respect him for that. His preference for the antique pen and paper had, perhaps, been a far more effective security measure than any number of firewalls, passwords or data encryption algorithms.

Perhaps the secret is in this study somewhere? A secret desk drawer? A fake book spine?

Deacon scanned the antique books along the shelves and the folders of data printouts stacked one atop the other. There was nothing for it; both he and Leonard were going to have to go through all of those to see whether Mason had hidden secret papers amongst them. He was beginning to get a feel for the old man, to get an idea of how his mind functioned. From interviews with the lab technicians that had worked closely with Mason, he had begun to discover many of the old man's idiosyncrasies, habits. Deacon got up and approached the book shelves and ran his finger along the ancient spines.

Mason fondly loved all things antique; hated all things modern. *Technology* in general. Strange for a man who worked in the field of genetics. Mason passionately hated computers. He much preferred to think with a pen in his hand. The ink blotter on his desk was testament to that, covered as it was with scribbles and scrawls, many faded by the years.

Deacon could understand the appeal of a fountain pen in one hand, almost as if the intelligence, the wisdom, lay inside the thing itself and the hand teased it out one idea at a time by wafting it closely over paper.

He approached a star chart of Human Space framed on the wall between the book shelves. It was a print he was familiar with, a popular one done in the style of ancient Old Earth maps, looking as if it had had been crafted by some medieval cartographer on papyrus.

He could imagine Mason standing before it studying it intently as he decided where best to send his creation. He could imagine that the old man must have stood right here, looking carefully at the groupings of stars and worlds and the main commercial routes between them for many hours, tracing the routes with his fingers, using his faithful fountain pen as a pointer.

A thought occurred to Deacon.

It was something he had noticed, when looking though some of the data printouts that Mason had read and commented on with his pen. If you held the printouts at an angle to the light, the black ink from Mason's fountain pen was a little glossier than the derma-jet print ink.

Deacon stood closer to the chart. He lent against the wall and looked obliquely across the star chart so that the glow of Pacifica's reflected light cast a dull blue sheen across the printed chart.

Oh my.

Glistening on the chart were several faint pen strokes. And the small casual swirl of a loop. With his head still pressed against the wall, he placed his finger on the chart in the middle of the loop Mason's pen had once upon a time inscribed and then pulled back to look squarely at it.

His finger obscured a world on the star chart. Hoping that it might have the same name as one of the five worlds Leonard had suggested, he pulled it away.

Harpers Reach.

It *was* one of them.

Mason, lost in deep concentration, must have run his pen casually across the dark printed surface of this chart, not aware that there was a discernible mark being left.

Deacon hurried back across to the desk and studied the list of requests that had come from Harpers Reach. Mason had checked out only sixty-three from this world over the last two decades.

Only sixty-three.

Not a horrendously large number. If he went there himself, with some additional manpower, it could be quickly done. Within a few weeks, he could easily locate each and every child and dispose of all of them. It would be much quicker and more discreet, and certainly more thorough, if he supervised this directly, rather than entrusting it to the local authorities on the world itself. They were bound to ask awkward questions and more than likely, they would screw the job up.

He stepped smartly out of Mason's study into his lab. Leonard was busy studying the list of a thousand names on another holo terminal.

'Leonard?'

'Yes…Deacon.'

'Harpers Reach. We need to make arrangements to head out there immediately.'

OMNIPEDIA:
[Human Universe digital encyclopaedia]

Article: 'The Administration'

The Administration governed Human Space for over seven hundred years. It was formed in the aftermath of the colonial war, a period of devastation and disruption that lasted for just over two hundred years. The colonial war was fought between Old Earth, together with the colonised worlds of the Solar System, and the hundreds of newly settled worlds outside of the Solar System. In the wake of faster than light drives, first pioneered in the 25th century, humans rapidly expanded their presence in the galaxy and many of the more suitable worlds quickly became settled, and mirroring a period of history from over a thousand years earlier, declared themselves independent from Earth government.

The war took a long time to escalate to a point where significant numbers of lives were lost. In fact, for over a hundred years it was a cold war, as both sides mobilized their resources. The worlds of the solar system under leadership from Old Earth took many decades to develop a military force capable of fighting at an interstellar level, whilst the new colonial worlds were busy forging a myriad of complicated alliances and readying their defences.

However, once the war began in earnest, within the space of fifty years several dozen planets had been permanently rendered uninhabitable and many, many billions of lives were lost. Fifty-six years after the first military campaign was launched, the loose alliance of newly colonized worlds was all but crushed, whilst Old Earth and the worlds of the Solar System were crippled economically by the cost of prosecuting the war.

And so, a peace accord was finally struck. A new form of government was formed called the Colonial Administration. This authority was based on Liberty, one of the first worlds to be colonised outside the Solar System, and would be designed to govern ALL of Human Space.

So began seven hundred years of relatively peaceful expansion, but at a significant cost.

The Administration was initially conceived as a temporary institution to put an immediate end to the war. It was intended only to govern until something else could be devised, that would meet the demands of the old as well as the new worlds.

The Administration, an un-elected body, remained in power much longer than it should have, and little by little ensured its own permanent future.

Major reforms, put in place by it, guaranteed that the political elite on Liberty would remain the ruling caste indefinitely. Reforms such as....the creation of the Colonial Army, supposedly formed to police Human Space but actually functioned as the Administration's military muscle; the Department for Genetic Analysis, which was set up to study UV-caused genetic mutations and sterility but in the end became a tool for monitoring and controlling population growth; the InterWorld Trading Standard which was designed as a set of guidelines to help corporations from different worlds conduct business on a level playing field, but in fact became a set of corporation-friendly laws that over-rode all local, planetary, laws.

By controlling the military, population distribution and commerce, the Administration had created an unassailable position. That is, until Ellie Quin finally arrived to turn history on its head.

User Comment > Omni-Anarchist

The administration was a bunch of fascist pigs. Like the Old Earth dictator guy with the funny moustache - Hippler. Peace-n-protein fans.

User Comment > Anonymous User

Duh. It's Hivvler, you complete bacteria.

User Comment > DigiUniversalDaily

Subscribe to DUD to get daily news streams delivered from across Human Space via broadband width sub-space channels.

Subscribe here: <u>DUD</u>

CHAPTER 15

'Hufty, it's me again. Things are not so rinky-dink for us right now; not exactly happy-clappy. You know we had those jobs that were paying quite well? The ones at StarBreaks? Well, guess what? We lost them. Crud…it was going alright for a while there. Jez and I were beginning to put some creds away, we were making our first steps towards getting out of here. Then it all went a bit wrong.'

'Jez was nearly arrested for hurling one of her deliveries at a law marshal. They came to visit the restaurant and cautioned Jez in front of our boss Mr Noah. And that was it, we were both of us kicked out there and then.'

'So…that happened a while ago. Then a few weeks back, we nearly got arrested for selling this drink that, as it turns out, can occasionally turn poisonous and kill you. I'm serious. Both me and Jez had some of it, a lot of it actually…thought it was great. But you know, it could have turned funny on us, and *blap* we could have been poisoned. So we had to stop selling it, and get rid of it. But that really cost us a lot of money, and we've been scraping by ever since.'

'We've both been trying as hard as possible to get some decent work. I mean, there is work out there and we've picked up and had a go at several jobs, but they just haven't been working out.'

Ellie stopped recording and looked out through the scuffed Perspex of the bubblestop. She watched a skyhound rise up from the streets below, slowly turning as it rose, its twin headlights casting powerful beams through the haze. On its flaking yellow painted roof, red and green navigation lights blinked in turn. She listened to the dull hum of the vehicle's thrusters as it gently drew nearer, the intensity of the noise gradually drowning out the ever present chaotic symphony of the city. She waited until it had made its final approach and nestled gently against the bubblestop before climbing aboard and making her way to the back of the vehicle.

'Jez's in a bad way. I've never seen her so low, so depressed. It's like she's given up. Mind you, I can't blame her. Nothing seems to have gone right for her since…well, since she met me, I guess. She lost that job at

Dantes, then at StarBreaks, then all that money we lost on that stupid drink that poisons you if it doesn't like you. It's just been hard because we're now behind on the rent, and we're playing catch-up. It's like this city is ganging up against us…or, I dunno, like New Haven is alive and doing everything it can to stop us leaving, to suck us back down.'

She sat at the back of the skyhound as it ascended with a hum of its thrusters, then, looked down at the glistening, shimmering carpet of the city below. For the first time she realised that the view didn't fill her with a sense of wonder or excitement. Not any more. The lustre was beginning to dull, the novelty of this new world beginning to wear off. It dawned on her that for the first time since arriving nearly six months ago, the city somehow felt smaller. It seemed like the enviro-dome had shrunk, and now she was beginning to feel as trapped as she had, once upon a time, sitting in her little agri-dome, Betsy, and staring up at the stars, the Veil and the flickering light of occasional star ships.

She felt like all she had done is exchange one plastic sky for another one.

Sucking us down.

Aaron was right. That's what the city did to you after a while. It was like some giant Venus flytrap. Yes, she nodded...that's exactly what it was like, some mean-spirited carnivorous plant; luring its prey in with a promise, and then snatching at you; trapping you and then slowly sucking you dry, digesting you bit by bit in its juices. Aaron had warned her something like this would happen.

And Jez had warned her too, after losing her job at Dantes. With hindsight, she realised that Jez's outburst weeks ago, had been her last cry of desperation, as she struggled frantically against the gravitational pull of the city. The trip to meet the fortune-teller with the penis-trunk, the StarBreaks job, and all the others in the last few weeks - all of that was Jez making her one last big effort to break free. And now it seemed like she had finally given up squirming and thrashing.

Now it was time to sit still and be digested.

It frightened her.

If Jez gave up the fight, Ellie wondered selfishly what would happen to her. She knew she couldn't survive here alone. Her friend had been the driving force for the two of them. Without Jez pushing them both onwards and upwards, they would both sink.

'The last job we both had at the Recyc-plant, Hufty, lasted only four days. And then Jez said she couldn't be bothered to do it any more. I covered for her for a couple of days, then they found out she hadn't been turning up for the shift, and she got kicked out. So, that was last week, and Jez's just been watching the toob since.'

Yesterday, Jez hadn't even bothered to put any clothes on. Ellie had left her and set out to catch a hound to take her to the Recyc-plant in the Industrial Sector and returned ten hours later to find Jez in the same position on the jel couch, still only in her underwear and her cleavage filled with synthipop crumbs, watching a cruddy off-world sopa-dram.

Ellie sighed forlornly, her breath spraying the window with an opaque cloud of condensation, which she smeared away with her fingers. 'The job I'm doing now is another daggy one, I'm afraid. I'm sorting through rubbish for recyclables. It's the only job I could get. And we need the money, so…got to do it really. I hope….'

Ellie paused her voice diary. She was going to say *I hope Jez snaps out of it soon.*

But unless something radical turned up, she couldn't see Jez suddenly jumping up out of the couch, dressing, and joining her to go and work over at the plant. Truth be told, Ellie couldn't see herself keeping it up for much longer. The pay was poor, the hours long and the work tedious.

'I'm sure it'll turn out for the best, Hufty. It's just a rough patch we're going through, that's all.'

With that she turned off the voice-diary and looked out of the window once more, as the grimy hues of the Industrial Sector loomed into view. She smiled though. At least there was something nice to look forward to before the start of today's shift. It had been too long, and she realised she had really missed him.

*

'Aaron!' she called out as she crossed the street towards the plastic seats and tables set out in front of the diner. Amidst the crowd of seated shuttle pilots enjoying a quick meal outside Dionysius's, she saw a mop of floppy fair hair turn one way then the other.

'Over here!' she called out again as she approached him.

Aaron sat upright and finally caught sight of Ellie. His broad face instantly creased with a grin. 'Hey! How are you girl?' his deep voice boomed, to the irritation of the other pilots sitting nearby. 'Sit down, and I'll get you a coffee.'

Ellie slumped down in a seat and watched him shuffle his way through the tables to the diner.

The gloom she had been feeling all last night had lifted.

She had failed to turn up here again the last time they were scheduled to meet. That made it three times in a row that she had stood him up; nine weeks in total since they had last sat here together. All day at work she had agonised over whether he would be here waiting for her one more time. She was almost certain that he wouldn't.

And she would only have herself to blame for that.

But here he was, just as he said he would; same place, exactly the same time....true to his word. Catching sight of the top of his scruffy head had been the tonic she most desperately needed. Seeing his tanned face, his craggy eyes, his tatty beard, and the crumpled beige boiler-suit that he seemed to live in all the time, was in a way like coming home.

Ellie clamped her lips together and felt her throat tighten. She felt like crying, but was damned if she was going to do that right in front of him.

Aaron returned from the diner carrying two steaming cups of coffee, squeezed himself through towards Ellie and sat down heavily in front of her.

'There you go girl,' he said. He studied her silently for a moment. 'I was getting really very worried about you,' he said finally. 'You stood me up last time and the time before. I was beginning to think that was it. No more Ellie Quin.'

Ellie struggled hard to keep the tears in. She nodded guiltily. It would be all too easy to let it out in front of him; to spill her worries over Jez, the lack of money, missing her home and family. Aaron would insist on taking her home there and then. And the thing was, feeling as she did right now, she would probably agree to go.

And then, her little voyage of self-discovery would be all over, and Jez would be left all alone to rot in that cube of theirs.

'I'm sorry Aaron. I….I've just been so busy,' she muttered guiltily.

'You look less…*dressy* this time,' he said pointing at her more practical clothing; baggy grey trousers and a faded red sweatshirt.

'They're my work clothes.'

'You still working in a diner?'

'No, it's…umm, it's factory work now.'

'Okay, well…that's good,' he said offering her an encouraging nod. 'Probably.'

'I don't wear my dressy clothes for work….it's mucky there.'

I don't wear them at all now. We've never two creds to spare for going-out fun.

'Sure. I can imagine turning up at a factory wearing what I saw you in last time wouldn't go down so well.'

Ellie offered a muted laugh. 'No, not really.'

'So how are you doing girl? You earning enough? You keeping up with your bills?'

'Yeah, of course.'

'How's your friend? Jez?'

'Jez? Oh yeah she's great. She's taking care of me,' Ellie said, the slightest wobble of emotion beginning to creep into her voice. She coughed, cleared her throat. 'We're having a fine old time.'

'Good,' said Aaron. He smiled and nodded and then took a sip of his coffee. 'Have you been keeping in touch with your folks?'

'Yes, I spoke with them a couple of weeks ago. I told them I was okay, doing alright in the city.'

Aaron studied her silently for a moment. 'Are you?' he asked.

'What?'

'Are you doing alright?'

'Yes, of course,' she replied a little too quickly.

Aaron studied her silently, as she made-busy, blowing at her coffee.

Ellie's struggling, it's written all over her face.

He knew, though, that she would never admit to it. This girl was too proud to let it slip that things weren't working out. And perhaps that's what he liked most about her. She had a strength of purpose, a will, an energy that you rarely saw in people these days. Lethargy and a sullen listlessness seemed to be the norm he noted, looking around. If there was any justice in this world, a bright young thing like Ellie would be doing far better than some crappy job in a factory. He wanted to help her out again, but he knew she wouldn't accept any charity, and anyway, he needed to watch his money now. The best he could do was to keep meeting her like this, keep an eye on her. But then, the way things were headed, he wasn't sure how much longer he'd be able to keep doing even that.

Ellie blew on her coffee, and then tested the temperature with her top lip. 'Thanks for the drink,' she said.

'S'alright.'

In turn she studied Aaron out of the corner of her eye as he looked around the plaza. He seemed different somehow, less jovial than usual. Well, at least less jovial than she remembered him being. He looked tired in fact. 'How's the shuttle business going then?'

Aaron shrugged. 'It's been better,' he said dismissively.

'Why? What's up?'

'No big deal…'

'What? I know you…*no big deal*, means it's a big deal. What's happened?'

Aaron laughed. 'You can read me that easily can you?'

Ellie frowned impatiently. 'Come on, tell me.'

The big man leant back in his chair and stroked his chin. 'Well, see...I've lost the Oxxon run.'

Ellie gasped. 'Why? What happened?'

'Undercut by a bigger haulage company. They're winding things down up there, cutting costs again...and I'm a part of that process.'

'But that's *most* of your business isn't it?'

Aaron nodded casually. 'A large chunk if it. Yeah, I suppose so.'

'What are you going to do?'

He looked around, up at the towers across the street. 'I dunno. I'll work something out.'

Aaron's reluctant glance at the industrial towers around them weren't wasted on Ellie.

'You're not thinking of selling up and moving into the city are you?'

'What? Hell no...of course not,' he replied awkwardly.

'Oh my crud, you are, aren't you?'

Aaron looked at her across the table. Ellie could see he was weighing up the answer. If he was even *considering* selling his beloved shuttle, *Lisa*, then things had to be pretty bad for him. She knew how much he despised the city and the sort of people who flocked into it. It would be the end of him if that was all he could do; sell up, move in and end up working some loader down by the port.

'Uh, no. I'm sure it'll work out alright. I'll find some other contracts out there.'

'There has to be, right? It's a big planet, things need to be transported around,' nodded Ellie.

'Yup. It's a big planet, there's always work. You don't need to waste time worrying about me young lady.'

Ellie took a sip of her coffee. She realised he was just as bad as her, tucking his woes away behind a shrug and a smile. They had that in common alright, stupid stubbornness. 'So, are you totally finished with the Oxxon refinery run, or do you have any more to do before it's over?'

'It's all done. I've got a green pad lined up for a few days, then hopefully I can get on to a black pad whilst I see if I can scare up some more business.'

Ellie recalled the colour-coded landing pads down at the port. The green pads were only for short term stays. The black pads were for long term stopovers, useful for Aaron while he needed to sort his business out, but expensive as they charged an extortionate occupancy fee per day.

Although it would be nice to know he was around; parked-up in New Haven, just a skyhound journey away from her for the immediate future, she found herself worrying about what would eventually become of him. She had no idea what his position was, whether he had creds saved up for a slack period like this to tide him over, or whether he was right on the edge. But unless he found some new business, eventually he would have to sell the shuttle for what he could get.

And then?

Ellie felt even more troubled now than she had on the way over.

First Jez had hit a *downer*, and now Aaron was looking like he was on his way out of business. Both of them were the sort of people she thought would have thrived in a tough world like this. They were both fighters, survivors. She envied them their bullet-proof self-confidence, their resilience…the fact that neither of them seemed to be plagued with self-doubt or low self-esteem, like she was. And yet, even *they* were struggling to find their way, to keep going.

She still held out hope, however, that Jez would bounce back with yet another audacious and impractical scheme to earn them enough money to escape New Haven; that for now she was just recharging her batteries, enjoying a week-long slob-out before readying herself for the next round. And that Aaron would quickly find his feet once more with another steady bread-and-butter shuttle run and everything would be back on track for all three of them.

Because the alternative was too depressing to contemplate. If neither Jez nor Aaron could hack it here in New Haven, what chance did a complete nothing like her have?

CHAPTER 16

Ellie entered the habi-cube to find Jez still hadn't moved.

'Hey Ell'....how's things?' she mumbled as she crammed the last of the soyo puffs into her face.

Ellie sat down beside her. 'I met Aaron earlier.'

'Aaron?...Oh right, the trucker guy?'

'Yeah.'

'He alright?' she asked distractedly.

Ellie nodded, not bothering to elaborate. On the way home aboard the skyhound her mind had been full of variants of a motivational speech she wanted to give Jez. There was little she could do to help Aaron, but the least she could do was try and pull Jez out of this downward slope of lassitude. A week on the couch surely was long enough, and she was worried that, unless something happened soon, they'd both be out on the street before Jez came to her senses.

'Jez, I don't want to sound like your mum, but-'

'So don't,' snapped Jez.

'…but, maybe it's time you got up and-'

'Ellie! I mean it! I don't need you to give me the big ra-ra speech, okay?'

She bit her lip, wondering whether it was wise to push the matter further. In the months they had lived together, they'd yet to have a real argument….well, at least a serious one. It looked as if right here, right now, was going to be the first true test of their friendship. Ellie knew there was never going to be a good time to do it; Jez needed this friendly kick in the ribs - the sooner, the better.

She sucked in a breath, and steadied her nerve before reaching out for the remote control and turning the toob off.

'Jez, you've got to pull yourself out of this…this…'

'This *what?* I don't need to pull myself out of anything thank you very much,' Jez snarled. 'And, what makes you so fregging great anyway? Huh? So, you've got a daggy job down the Recyc? Double-rah for you. The money's so crud it barely pays for the 'hound over there and back anyway!'

'But it's *something* Jez. We need to bring in something.'

'What's the fregging point? Every job we've had isn't anywhere near enough to get us off this crap-stack. Even if we could save every last cred, it'll take us years and years.'

'We need money right now otherwise we'll be on the street!'

'So what? That's where I found you, so you'll be no worse off will you?'

Ellie was taken aback. Where the crud had *that* come from? There was a really nasty, spiteful tone behind those words. 'What are you saying, Jez?'

'I'm saying, you're a waste of space Ellie....you drippy-chik. I'm saying that since I pulled you up out of the gutter all those weeks ago, nothing has gone right for me. Nothing!'

Ellie felt her heart freeze, and her stomach twisted itself into a knot. 'Why are you being so shitty? Why are you saying this?'

'Why? I don't know. Maybe because I think you're holding me back. Maybe because you're just bad luck. Maybe because I'm fed up carrying your precious little self on my back all the time,' Jez said reaching out for the toob's remote control. 'I'm not your mum, or your big sister, I wasn't put on this fregging planet to wipe shit off your arse for you. Maybe I'm just worn out being your cruddy babysitter!'

'Oh,' said Ellie.

Jez cycled through the stations in silence and Ellie watched various holographic images flicker on in front of her, and then vanish to be replaced by another.

Jez's words reverberated in the silence. The volume on the toob was turned down.

So expertly handled, Ellie girl.

She got up and headed towards her cube. Jez was right, of course. She always was. She was the one who came up with all the big ideas, she was the momentum that had carried them both forwards. Maybe Jez would be better off without her to slow her down. The only thing Ellie had brought along to the party was some naive fantasy to get off-world, but then Jez had wanted that too - once upon a time, at least. All Ellie could take credit for is accidentally re-awakening that desire in Jez. That's all she'd managed to do.

She entered her cube, the door closed behind her, and the small light above her bed flickered and winked on. She sat down on the bed and looked out of the small round porthole beside her pillow at the city below.

Maybe it's time to think about going back home.

Aaron had suggested he might try his luck over at Harvest City. It was a much smaller domed city, but there might be some business he could pick up ferrying goods between there and New Haven. It was a long shot, but unless he found some other work here, it was something he would have to at least try. He told Ellie that if he did head across to Harvest, he could take her with him and drop her off home; it was not very far out of the way.

Ellie had said no, flatly, very sternly. An hour ago, talking with Aaron, she wouldn't even have considered the idea. Now...seeing how Jez *really* felt about her, she wondered whether it might be an idea to take Aaron up on his offer. She felt the very first tear trickle down her left cheek and run into the corner of her mouth.

That's the price you pay for putting all of your trust in one person.

She realised now that she had probably leaned too much on Jez. Her friend wasn't really to blame. She was. And Jez was right about that other thing - ever since Jez had picked her up off the floor things *really* hadn't gone right for her.

Ellie pulled up a corner of her quilt and blew her nose, then wiped her eyes. It was time to admit she was beaten; at least for now. Maybe in a few years time, when she was a little older, wiser, smarter she might try again. To be fair, she was still just a child. Twenty yes, but really just a child. There were, of course, other children in New Haven, but they were not on their own, they had their families. It was unfair of Ellie to rely on Jez to be a substitute parent or an older sister.

She could try again in a few years, there was no law that said you only get one chance to try and break free. She could try…

There was a knock on the door, and she heard Jez's muffled voice. 'Ellie?'

Ellie remained silent. She wasn't ready just yet to talk to Jez. But Jez persisted, knocking again. 'Ellie, open the door….don't force me to say *please,* because, as you know, I don't do *please*.'

She clamped her lips tightly shut and concentrated on the view out of her window.

'Okay, then….I'll say what I've got to say through this door. Listen, I'm really sorry. I…I said things just then I don't really mean. I genuinely didn't mean any of that crud I said. Not a word of it.'

The headlights of a passing air car fleetingly lit up Ellie's small room as it swooped by.

'In fact Ellie, here's a funny thing. I need you just as much you need me. You've helped me remember that there's much more out there than this cruddy place. And I love you for that.'

Ellie continued to stare out of the window, she watched a holographic advert slide into view. It was an ad for ProtYum ice cream.

'And we *are* a good team. You're the brains, I'm the brawn. So, look. I'm all done being defeatist and miserable and I'm ready for us to get back on the deal, and work our way out of here.'

Ellie watched the advert drift lazily across the night sky. A young, beautiful, pale-skinned family seemingly, without a care in the world, were frolicking in snow, hurling snowballs at each other, whilst all effortlessly enjoying tubs of tasty, nutritious ProtYum.

Outside, Jez rested her head against the door with a dull thump. 'So, Ellie….I'm sort of done talking to the door now. Please - there you made me say it - *please* open the door and tell me you forgive me.'

Nice one Jez, you really know how to charm people, dontcha?

Jez ground her teeth with frustration. She had said some pretty cruddy things to Ellie, and the stupid thing was she hadn't meant it, even as it was tumbling out of her mouth. It was just frustration. She was angry that nothing she did ever seemed to make any damned fregging difference. She was still no closer to getting off this cruddy planet than she was five years ago when she'd first arrived in the city. It was like every effort you made, *everything* that you did merely managed to keep your head above water and no more. And that's all you could ever hope to achieve in New Haven. And if by some miracle you did manage to earn just a little more than you needed to pay the rent, the O2 bill, and the groceries, then the temptation was all around you to go and splash out on some shiny little bauble of distraction. Those temptations were everywhere; on every toob channel, on every wall - adverts cajoling you to spend, spend sp...

The door slid open and Jez nearly toppled in. 'Ah thank crud, I'm really...'

Ellie shushed her with a finger and then said, 'Jez, I have just had the most *incredible* idea!'

CHAPTER 17

They entered the main entrance of the shopping mall, Nimods, the largest in New Haven. Ellie looked up at the lift column in the centre of the mall's central atrium, rising twenty floors upwards and another ten down into the ground.

'Wow,' she muttered.

Surrounding the central space of the atrium she could see the smooth cream-coloured balustrades of each of the floors, receding up into the distance. Unlike the streets of the city, Nimods Mall had a cool, soothing ambience. The ever present crush of pedestrian traffic, the flickering neon brashness and the noise of countless sky vehicles and floating billboards, was left mercifully outside.

'Have I not shown you round this place yet?' asked Jez.

'Nope.'

'Hmmm, sorry about that. Mind you it is oober-pricey in here. You'd get a much better price down at Baldini's Bazaar on anything you see in here.'

Ellie stepped towards a map of the mall and ran her finger down the names of the businesses plying their trade inside.

'Look, are you going to tell me where exactly you're dragging me along to Ellie?' asked Jez yet again.

'Not yet,' she replied. She found the name of the place she had agreed to meet him at. 'McGuires'. It was a bar on the eleventh floor, about half way up. It had been *his* suggestion; he'd obviously been there himself before. Jez spotted where Ellie's finger had come to a stop.

'Ahh McGuires? I heard it's quite trooby inside. Very olde-worlde style. But why exactly are we going there, girl?

They took one of the central lifts up to the eleventh, all the while Ellie's eyes drank in the tidy, calming pastel splendour of the floors as they rose past them.

'For crying out loud Ellie, when are you going to tell me what this *Big Idea* of yours is all about?' Jez asked again as they stepped out of the lift, and made their way across a shiny faux-marble floor towards the glowing neon sign of McGuires bar across the way.

She stopped outside the entrance. 'This is it.'

'Hey. Did you get a job here?' asked Jez incredulously. 'That's pretty impress-'

'No,' said Ellie, 'no job. We're meeting someone in here.'

'Who?! Who the frag do you know that I don't?'

Ellie led the way inside. McGuires was dimly lit. The walls looked like they were clad with a dark oak mock-wood panelling, and fake oil lamps spaced along the walls glowed, warming the inside with an amber hue. She looked around. The bar had many dimly-lit, high-panelled booths with green faux-leather benches tucked snugly inside them around what looked like old wooden barrels. Ellie had seen barrels like these in an old histo-dram on the toob....something to do with pirates and big wooden boats with sails.

She spotted him sitting impatiently in one of the booths, just about to finish off a tall fluted glass of beer.

'Jez, this way.'

She led her friend towards the booth, and at the last moment Aaron looked up at them. 'Well Ellie-girl, it's good to see you again so soon, but is there any chance you gonna tell me what the hell this is all about now?'

'Yes, of course,' she said a little nervously.

Ellie had told neither of them what her great idea was. Just that she had one she thought might solve a lot of problems all round. She knew it would sound kind of cruddy if she just blurted it out without taking the time to think how to *present* it to both of them. Keeping it to herself despite Jez's incessant cajoling and pestering over the last twenty-four hours, had given her a bit more time to think through how she'd sell the idea to them.

Also, adding an air of mystery to the Big Idea had made Jez really sit up and take notice. Curiosity had been driving her to distraction. Jez was becoming annoying in fact, pestering constantly over the last day as Ellie set up this meeting. Ellie half suspected Jez would be ready to sign up to anything just to find out what the frag the big secret was.

Of course, the person she *really* needed to sell this to was Aaron. Without him this was going nowhere.

'Aaron, this is my friend I told you about,' she said stepping to one side revealing Jez.

His eyebrows shot up briefly as he took in her tall athletic figure clad in a crimson pvc corset, the yellow and black striped leggings, and glo-boots that pulsated with a neon orange light around the ankle.

'Jez, this is my friend, Aaron.'

Aaron nodded politely, 'yes you're very much how I imagined you'd look.' He reached out a large hand, which she grabbed firmly and shook.

'And you're almost how I imagined you'd look,' she replied a little coolly.

Ellie grinned. 'Great, introductions all done.'

Jez sat down opposite Aaron, studying him with the slightest hint of distaste betrayed by the curl of her lips. Aaron sat up straight and stretched his back. 'So Ellie, you got me all the way over here…you want to tell me what this is about, girl?'

'Yeah,' said Jez impatiently, 'I'm all a ga-ga with this big mystery.'

Ellie sat down on a stool and looked at both of them in turn over the top of the plastic barrel. She licked her lips nervously, hoping she wasn't about to make a big fool of herself.

Ok girl, let's not mess this one up.

'It's just an idea I had. I think it's something that might help all three of us out.

But first, should we just get something to drink?'

Jez nodded, 'sure, it's been a while since I've had one. In fact it's been too long since I had one anywhere. Three Spartans?'

Aaron shook his head, 'I'll have a bottle of Genesis.'

He pulled some creds out of the breast pocket of his boiler suit. 'My buy. I know you girls are a little short right now.'

Jez grabbed the money quickly, offered Aaron a sugary smile, and turned and headed towards the bar. Aaron watched her go and then turned to Ellie. 'So that's the infamous Jez then.'

'What do you think of her?' she asked.

'Hmm....she's no shrinking violet.'

'What does that mean?'

'She's not shy.'

Ellie shook her head, 'oh, she's definitely not that.'

There was a question she needed to ask him before she took things any further. 'So, have you found any other work yet?'

Aaron shook his head grimly. 'I checked with the port agents...there's nothing around right now. All the cross-planet contracts are covered. Unless something turns up soon, I'm going to have to take that gamble and go across to Harvest to see if I can pick anything up there.'

Ellie nodded, she was genuinely disappointed for Aaron, but at the same time guiltily relieved that it meant the Big Idea hadn't been shot down just yet.

Jez returned with three bottles clasped together in her hands.

'You got served quick,' said Aaron. 'Took me ages to get any attention from behind the bar.'

Jez shrugged. 'It helps if you've got a pair of titties to jiggle.'

Aaron smiled, 'fair point.' He liked her candour.

Jez set the bottles down on the barrel. They all reached for their drinks, and then both Aaron and Jez slowly turned in unison towards Ellie.

'Well?' said Aaron.

Here goes. Get it right, girl.

'Right then...this is my big idea.' She cleared her throat apprehensively. 'We sell shuttle trips up to the north polar region to rich people in New Haven who have never seen real snow.'

Aaron and Jez stared at her in silence.

'That's my idea.'

The silence lengthened as both of them continued to stare at her. Then, after a few moments, she noticed Aaron's eyes darted upwards, focusing on some distant point above her. She smiled, knowing exactly what he was doing. He was calculating something in his head; probably fuel burn to the polar region and back.

Jez on the other hand looked puzzled by something more elementary. 'What's 'snow'?'

'White stuff, like ice...but soft. Some planets have whole areas covered in the...'

'Oh that! I've seen that on Friends and Lovers,' she said and then paused. 'My God, we have that *stuff* on Harpers Reach?'

Ellie nodded. 'Yeah, right up near the north pole.'

'Thousands of square miles of it,' added Aaron before returning to some obscure calculation in his mind.

'You're kidding? Crud! Who would've thought this crappy mud ball would have something that fantasto on it?'

'That was what I thought when I first saw it.'

'You've been there?' Jez asked incredulously.

'Yes. It was lovely. Aaron was doing a run up to the O2 refineries there. We stopped on the snow, got out and played around on it.'

'OhMyCrud! That's just so….so…'

'Cool?'

Jez nodded, taking a slug of her Spartan. Aaron, temporarily put whatever it was that he was calculating to one side and re-engaged with them. 'So Ellie, how do we all fit into this idea of yours then?'

'Well,' she tapped her fingers, 'you've got a shuttle. Jez is a sales genius. She can sell anything to virtually anyone. And me? Well I could do all the other things that aren't piloting a shuttle or selling.'

He leant forward onto the barrel, placing a big elbow on its plastic surface and cradling his bristly chin in one hand. From what Ellie could read in his body language, he was definitely giving the proposition a few moments of consideration. 'The thing is Ellie, *Lisa* is a transport shuttle. There's no room in the cockpit for passengers, and to be honest, it's all a bit grubby and…'

'But there's room in the cargo hold.'

Aaron nodded, 'true. But we can't put people in there!'

'If it was hosed down and given a good scrub, a coat of paint, some carpet on the floor and if we fixed in some bunks, some chairs and a FoodSmart....?'

He nodded slowly, 'Well...I suppose...yeah, maybe.'

Jez leant forward, 'and what? I sell the tickets?'

Ellie looked at Jez anxiously, wondering whether she was being too pushy. Jez was the one used to handing out the orders. 'Um, yeah....what do you think?'

Her dark sculpted eyebrows knotted as she stared long and hard at Ellie. She slammed her bottle down on the barrel noisily. 'I think that's a fregging brilliant idea!'

'This would take some money, Ellie,' cautioned Aaron. 'We'll need to do a bit more than throw a bit of paint around. We need to install an O2 system in the hold, and run a power cable through for lighting and the FoodSmart.'

'And we'd need to work out how we sell these trips,' added Jez. 'Some advertising. You know? Leaflets or something, maybe even a counter or something down near the port!'

Ellie nodded agreement with both of them. 'Yeah, I know. It's stuff we have to do first. I didn't say it was going to be easy. But I think between us…? You know?'

Aaron and Jez looked at each other silently. Ellie smiled as the first teasing buzz of excitement tickled her spine. Those weren't objections they were both voicing, they were the first tentative steps towards a serious brainstorming.

Crud...I think they like it.

'That's all gonna take money, Ellie,' said Aaron.

'I know, and neither Jez nor I can offer any help at all with that,' she replied meekly.

'But,' Jez stepped in, 'we can work hard, both me and Ellie can. For nothing, you know, until we start making some money that is.'

Aaron studied them both. 'I'm sure you're both hard workers, but whilst you're earning nothing, how are you going to keep a cube over your heads?'

Ellie looked at him. 'I was thinking….?'

'Oh, no! I'm not too sure that's a good idea ladies. It was bad enough with just us two bunking in there, Ellie. I'm not sure I can cope with another one bunking in the shuttle with me.'

'It wouldn't be for long. Just as soon as we start making money, Jez and I could find somewhere else to live.'

'But, what about during the trips up to the polar region and back?'

'Well, you're going to want us girls on board to look after the passengers, aren't you? You're the pilot, we'll be the stewardesses.'

'Just like Abigail Swifty in Shuttle Stop 7,' added Jez, 'we could have a uniform and everything! Ahh, that would be properly-mint. What do you think Ellie-girl? Our own uniforms?'

Ellie kept her mind on the practical issues that Aaron was focusing on. 'I suppose we could find space in the cargo area to section off as stewardess quarters. It really depends on how much passenger space we need, and how much we can charge them.'

Aaron shuffled uncomfortably on the bench. 'That's right Ellie. And that's what really will decide if this is going to make us any money at all. To work out how much fuel we'd burn, I need to know how much weight we're carrying. And only when we know that would we know how much we'd need to charge someone for a trip up there. And even then, there's no knowing if anybody will want to spend money on a trip like that.'

'You're kidding right?' said Jez.

Aaron shook his head sincerely, 'I'm not big on joking.'

'No, he's not, really,' agreed Ellie.

'Agghh...just a figure of speech,' said Jez. 'No what I'm saying is, I *know* people will pay a lot to see something like that. It's just far too cool.'

'While it lasts,' he muttered.

'What's that?'

Ellie explained. 'It's melting. In the next fifty years or so it'll all go as the world warms up.'

Jez spread her hands. 'Even better! If it's going to be gone one day, we could charge even more. Say....lemmesee...say two hundred creds, there and back? How does that sound?'

'Two hundred creds? You think there's enough people in this city who can spend two hundred creds on something like that?' Aaron asked.

'I'd say so. *Most* people...frankly, no. They're like me and Ellie, struggling to keep up with the bills. But you look up at the sky, and count the number of air cars. Anyone who lives up above the highest plaza levels, in the top ten-twenty floors of the tenement towers - they're the sort of people who can,' replied Jez. 'Crud, we could charge maybe three hundred creds a head from those sorts of bubble-heads.'

Ellie looked up at Aaron. 'And how many people could we get into that cargo hold, comfortably? Ten? Fifteen?'

Aaron locked his eyes on her as he quickly did the maths in his head. 'Minus fuel - say seven hundred creds fuel burn there and back,' he looked up at Jez and back to Ellie, 'that's two thousand three hundred creds profit for each trip.'

'Minus some other costs, like food and drink,' she added.

'Two thousand then.'

'Two thousand,' Jez repeated, with eyes as wide as saucers.

'And you should have most of that,' said Ellie to Aaron. 'Jez and I, could do with...' *Don't be greedy girl.*'...three hundred and fifty each?'

Aaron laughed. 'Three hundred and fifty!?'

'Alright, then maybe that's too much. What do you think about three hundred?' Ellie asked wincing slightly.

Aaron continued to laugh, and then slapped a big hand down on her arm. 'I was going to suggest four hundred each, Ellie girl. If I'm making a thousand profit with each trip, then I'm one happy-pappy.'

Jez spurted out a mouthful of her Spartan. '*Four* hundred! Crud, that's twice what I was earning at Dantes!'

The three of them stared at each other in silence. Aaron spoke quietly. 'That's IF…we can sell tickets at three hundred creds a go.'

Ellie and Jez nodded eagerly.

'Look let me think about this for a moment. It's all a lot to take in.'

'Of course,' replied Ellie. 'It was just an idea to think about. I'm sure one of us will find a very good reason why it can't be done. For sure.'

Aaron excused himself and went to the toilet.

Jez watched him go before turning back to Ellie and slapping her back proudly. 'My my,' she said, 'you're a clever little one aren't you?'

'It all depends on what he thinks though, Jez. It's *his* shuttle, *his* money, *his* risk. If it all falls flat, we're no worse off than we are now. But for Aaron, it's game over. It's taken him years of hard work to end up with that shuttle of his. What do you think of him by the way?'

'He seems okay so far. Not creepy like most older guys. How old is he anyway?'

Ellie realised she hadn't a clue. At a guess she would put him in his mid-thirties. But it was so hard to even guess. 'To be honest I haven't ever asked him.'

'I think I'd want to work on his presentation skills a bit. You know, if he's going to be our skipper. The soiled brown boiler suit just doesn't work for me, especially the stains…uh-uh,' she said with a grimace.

Ellie laughed, 'I'm sure we'll come to that at some point.'

'And what's his shuttle like anyway?'

'Well, it's not exactly like the ones you've seen on the toob.'

'You mean it's a rust bucket?'

Ellie waggled her hand, 'might need a little love and attention on the outside as well as the inside.'

'Hmmm, sounds like a lot of work there before we can get earning some creds.'

'But, we'd all be our own bosses, Jez….we'd be *business partners*.'

Jez perked up and smiled, she very much liked the sound of that. 'Business partners, eh?' she repeated.

'It's got to be better than slaving away for someone else,' Ellie continued. 'Every hour we put into it, is for us three, not someone else.'

Jez nodded in agreement. 'Crud, I hope he says yes to your idea, which by the way makes you officially überbrain-chik of our little team.'

Ellie laughed. 'Like you said, I'm the brains, you're the beauty. And anyway, if Aaron decides to do this, it'll be the three of us on the team.'

*

Aaron stood in the uni-gender pod and stared at his reflection in the mirror.

Am I going to do this?

He got the impression Ellie and her friend, Jez, had decided it all rather felt like a done deal. But the fact was, there was one hell of a lot at stake here. He'd been running the Oxxon deliveries for nearly fifteen years, saving every spare cred he had earned in order to finally have enough to own the shuttle outright. And since buying it, he had continued living frugally, most of the time aboard his beautiful *Lisa*, to save on an unnecessary rent. He had assumed, foolishly as it turned out, that the Oxxon contract would last long past his lifetime, that it would be a reliable contract for the rest of his working life - another thirty to forty years. But then those soulless, suited, corporation dittoheads had placed their business with someone else, and that was that.

There was virtually nothing surface-based heading into and out of New Haven. Everything the city required in terms of supplies came in from off-world via the port. Harvest City, on the other hand, had a much smaller port, and although most of what it needed came in off-world, there was also a trickle of supplies running across world from New Haven. But he knew most of that business was sucked up by the same damned haulage firm that had taken his Oxxon contract.

If he kept looking, he'd find *something,* right? There had to be other contracts out there. It was early days yet. All he had done so far was check in with the port agent and he had enough savings tucked away to burn for at least three months on a black pad before he needed to hit the panic button.

This idea of Ellie's, however, it sounded good. But there'd be a lot of work that would need to be done on the shuttle, and the thought of giving up his private space to fit in *both* girls; the laundry chaos, the giggling and larking around, the fact that it was small enough as it was with just him living in the cockpit . Between them they'd drive him mad.

But, the money could be great.

That was true if Ellie's friend, Jez, was right, if there *were* plenty of people out there who would pay good money to goof around in real snow. She seemed to have street-smarts enough to know what's hot and what's not in New Haven. But it was a big gamble, a *huge* gamble; he could blow all of his savings turning his shuttle into a prissy little pleasure cruiser only to find that no-one was interested enough to shell-out for a ticket.

On the other hand, it could earn them all enough to find a way off-world.

He knew Ellie wanted that, she'd said Jez wanted it too. And Aaron longed to transport his surface shuttle to a world much younger, and less tamed than this one and ply his trade there. It might be the one and only chance all three of them had.

Well, it might, but then again, it might just ruin me.

He decided he had wasted enough time mulling this damned thing over. It was a nice idea, a clever idea even, but he knew the haulage game. That's what he knew. Not the damned tourist business.

'This is completely crazy,' he muttered as he shook himself off.

The pleasure cruise game was for some other sucker. On this occasion, he had to let caution rule. His mind was settled. He washed his hands and left the soothing marine-blue calm of the uni-gender pod, working out how he was going to let the girls down as gently as possible. Destroy their dream. Pop their bubble.

'Sorry girls…this is just too impractical…' he practiced under his breath.

And no batting of eyelids or impassioned pleading was going to change his mind on this. It was too crazy. Too risky. This was *his* money. His retirement fund. The Lisa was literally all he had and young Ellie's fanciful plan was going to end up with him being as broke as those two girls back in the bar.

No way. Absolutely. No way am I going along with this crazy-stupid idea.

To be continued…..

In

ELLIE QUIN BENEATH THE NEON SKY
(Book 3 of the Ellie Quin Series)

It's one big, crazy universe out there.
Travel light.

ELLIE
QUIN vol.3

BENEATH THE NEON
SKY

ALEX SCARROW

ELLIE QUIN BENEATH THE NEON SKY
(Book 3 in the Ellie Quin series – available NOW)

Ellie and Jez's plans to escape the suffocating grasp of New Haven finally look like they may be successful. They're making money now, lots of it…but then, as always seems to be the way for Ellie, nothing ever goes entirely to plan.

The Administration's hatchet man has arrived.

ALSO BY ALEX SCARROW

Time travel is already happening, there are already people coming through from our future into our past…and they are corrupting it, contaminating it. But, a small covert agency has been set up to preserve our history and our timeline: the **TimeRiders**.

Embark on a profoundly exciting journey through history with this nine book series published by Puffin. Available on Amazon Kindle, iBookstore, and in print in all good book stores.

Printed in Great Britain
by Amazon.co.uk, Ltd.,
Marston Gate.